**Black Authors Ink Presents**

# THE OTHER LEVEL

## Dyshum M. Jones
## N.T.P

The Other Level

Copyright © 2020 Dyshum Jones

Interior Design: BlackAuthors Ink
Cover Design: Black Authors Ink

ISBN-13: 978-0-9971572-6-0

First Black Authors INK trade paperback edition 2020
Printed in the United States of America

Black Authors INK
5615 Memorial Drive Unit 802C
Stone Mountain, GA 30083

# Synopsis

Jesus Gormez, a powerful Mexican drug lord, known as one of the biggest cocaine and heroine suppliers to ever touch the United States. With a history of causing blood shed, he placed fear across the United States including other powerful men. Many have tried his gangsta status and have failed, costing them their lives in the process.

Gormez is tested when his nephew, Pedro Gormez is robbed and murdered in one of Jesus' stash houses in Greenville, SC. The murder of Pedro Gormez set in motion AK chopping, pistol's popping, and bodies dropping throughout the streets of Greenville. Jesus and the Gormez family declared with their last breath, that they would bring those responsible for Pedro's murder to a slow painful death.

Jesus is forced to utilize his many connects beginning with street hustlers and even crooked police officers. Having the long arm of the law on his side, Gormez is able to track down the killers of his nephew. Will Jesus and the Gormez crime family succeed in retaliating Pedro's death?

Tyson, the master mind of the NTP family, orchestrated the plan to rob Pedro, when Pedro tested the NTP's family gansta status, which resulted in Pedro's death. The NTP family is now forced to utilize their wits by exercising strategies, monopolizing precise timing, and calculating every step; all for the survival of the NTP family against the wrath of Jesus Gomez.

Tyson and the NTP family are up against all odds, staying ahead of the game and below the radar, trying to shift the burden of responsibility, all while nipping all weak links that may lead back them. Tyson, by any means necessary, will do whatever it takes for the survival of the NTP family. Will the NTP family survive Jesus Gomez's wrath?

Agent Johnson, of the Federal Bureau of Investigation, has been deep undercover in the Gormez family operation for five years. Posing as a crooked police officer, in the Greenville County Police Department, on Jesus' payroll, providing and leaking information to the Gormez family, in an attempt to obtain indictments on several members of the Gomez family and bring them to justice. However, Agent Johnson, finds himself in the middle of a mini war between the NTP and Gomez family while undercover. Will Agent Johnson be exposed as the mole in the hole, or will he bring the Gomez family to Justice?

# THE OTHER LEVEL

## CHAPTER 1

A black nine millimeter exploded releasing a slug straight through a young Mexican male's head, sending him smashing into the wall, and killing him instantly. As the Mexican slid down the wall, Chris shouted, "Oh shit!"

"What the fuck!" Tyson shouted while leveling a heated stare towards Joey.

"He was reaching, dog!" Joey yelled back. "I had to, he was reaching!"

Everyone could feel and hear the panic in Joey's voice as his adrenaline was pumping like a locator train barreling out of Savannah, Georgia on a hot summer day. The men turned their attention to the body and saw the Mexican's slight grip on his chrome .45 Magnum. It did appear that the guy was trying to make a play for his gun. If that was his plan, thank God he failed.

"Y'all said that nobody was gonna get hurt." Chris stated, panicking and pacing back and forth, rubbing his head.

"Shut the fuck up, Chris!" Dantwan bucked at Chris.

"Man, I'm not going down for this." Chris fiddled with the toothpick that hung from the corner of his mouth.

"Calm down, man." Tyson walked over to Chris, firmly placing his hands on his shoulders trying to help his nervous partner gain some composure.

"Aye man, he was reaching." Joey stated again, trying to reassure everybody that he had to shoot the Mexican.

Unconvinced that Chris was cool, Tyson waved his hand to get the groups undivided attention. "Look, everybody just chill for a minute, and let me think." He said in a stern chilled tone as the large vein in his neck flexed as he spoke.

"Why Chris always acting like a bitch?" Dantwan stated with disgust and disconnect in his tone, furious by Chris' cowardly behavior.

"Fuck that shit you talking, y'all said nobody was gone get hurt!" Chris bucked at Dantwan.

"Everybody shut the fuck up and let me think for a minute!" Tyson shouted again in rage.

Thirty-seconds floated by which felt like two hours.

"Yo Dantwan?" Tyson barked.

"Yeah what's up?" Dantwan quickly snarled back, not relinquishing eye contact with Chris.

"Start putting the money in the backpacks and the drugs in the trash bag. Tyson instructed.

"Joey?"

"What?" Joey responded and you could still hear the panic in his voice from blasting the Mexican.

"Help me wrap this wetback up in this rug. And Yo Chris?"

"Yeah." Chris sucked his teeth, acting nonchalant.

Check the windows and back doors to see if anybody out there." Tyson stated leaning over the dead Mexican's body dragging him onto the rug.

"Man I don't got nothing to do with this." Chris tried to enforce. Forgetting that the hands of one is the hands of all in the state of South Carolina and in the NTP family.

"Hold the fuck up just on minute. What the fuck you talking about nigga? Dantwan shouted, walking towards Chris with his hands balled into a fist.

"Lower y'all fucking voice before someone hear y'all. Chill the fuck out! Check this, here's what we gone do," Tyson begins to explain, "All of us are going to put a bullet in this wetback. If one of us goes down, we all go down together."

"Nigga, have you lost your rabbit ass mind? I haven't murked nobody." Chris blurted out.

"Nigga, if you don't shut the fuck up with that bitch shit." Dantwan said walking towards Chris again ready to knock the shit out of him but Tyson grabbed Dantwan.

"Hold up Dantwan, this how its gonna go down. Tyson put four slugs in a Glock. We're going to pass this around and one by one everybody put a bullet in this dead wetback. Now do y'all understand?" Tyson scorned.

"I'm with you Ty. Dantwan spoke up first, eager to show his loyalty to his crew.

"I'm already in deep." Joey stated while everybody turned towards Chris waiting for him to agree but Chris stared into space.

"Chris! Tyson yelled, Getting angrier by the second.

"Yeah, I guess I'm down." Not meaning one word of it.

Tyson screwed a silencer on the barrel of the gun. Then passed it to Dantwan. Dantwan grabbed the gun out of Tyson's hand, cocked it sending one of the slugs to the chamber. He aimed at the Mexican and squeezed the trigger. Blood and brain tissue splattered on the wall.

Dantwan then handed the Glock nine to Joey. And without hesitation he put another slug in the dead Mexican's chest. A thick blob of blood squirted out of his mouth and nose. Then Joey turned to Chris and handed him the gun. Chris grabbed the gun, pointed, aimed, then closed his eyes. The crew patiently waited but still after ten-seconds Chris failed to squeeze the trigger.

"I can't do it man!" Chris screamed.

Tyson snatched the gun out of Chris's hand and pointed, aimed, and squeezed the trigger, sending a slug into the Mexican's face, knocking half of his face off. Tyson immediately turned the gun on Chris pointing it at his head, "If you're not with us, you're against us." He squeezed the trigger, letting a bullet rip through Chris's forehead, killing him instantly.

"What you do that for?" Joey yelled hysterically while wiping blood splatter off of his face.

"I'll explain later but right now we have to move. Let's get outta here!"

Dantwan snatched the backpack off Chris with no remorse for his dead body.

"Joey help me move these trash bags to the back door." Tyson ordered, running back and forth to the window looking through the cracks of the curtains.

"What about the bodies?" Dantwan asked.

"Torch it!" Tyson dragged the trash bags filled with drugs to the back door.

Dantwan went to the kitchen to see what he could find to create a fire with. He grabbed the newspaper off the breakfast table and turned on the gas stove. To make sure the fire blazed he grabbed the cooking oil and poured it on the carpet and curtains in the living room. He then lit the newspaper on fire, tossing it onto the carpet.

As the flames spread throughout the house, the crew minus one, excited the back door. They jumped a couple of fences and came through an old woman's backyard on a dark side street. They jumped into the U-Haul truck, rented by a crack head in exchange for some blow. Thirty minutes later the crew pulled into the driveway of a one-bedroom shack house. They exited the U-Haul truck and walked through a side door, entering a small kitchen, connected to the living room.

Tyson and his crew threw the two trash bags filled with drugs in the corner of the room and then they began dumping the four large backpacks filled with money on the small kitchen table.

"That's what I'm talking about!" Dantwan yelled at the top of his lungs, hyped from pulling off the robbery.

"Calm down boys, this shit ain't over yet. I still have loose ends to tie up." Tyson informed the two men sitting around the table preparing to count and split their earnings.

"Man I don't feel right about this man." Joey stated with his head down to his chest.

"All this money and coke and you don't feel right, you better hit you a line then." Dantwan replied laughing, while dumping the last backpack filled with money on the kitchen table.

"Its not even that dog." Joey replied, wondering how he was going to explain Chris's death to Ms. Hill.

"Then what is it Joe?" Tyson asked with concerns, although he knew what the problem was.

"Did you?" He paused, "I mean, Did we have to kill Chris?"

"Nigga, don't start that shit, if it weren't for your trigger happy ass, Chris would still be alive." Dantwan replied while playing with the money resting on the table.

"I told you he was reaching for his gun, man."

"And you did the right, Joey, because had the Mexican got a shot off, one of us could be laying back there dead in that burning house, Tyson stated.

"I know man but did we have to kill Chris?" Joey asked hurting inside because his best friend was dead.

"Fuck that nigga." Dantwan blurted out not giving a fuck about Chris since he acted weak during crunch time.

"Nah Dantwan man! Ain't no fuck Chris. Joey and Chris go way back like Levis and shell toe Adidas, plus I loved Chris too but he wasn't with us. Listen, ain't none of us diving slow into the belly of the beast living the rest of our lives in prison and Chris was the key that was going to lock those prison gates behind us. Do you understand?" Tyson asked with bass in his voice.

"When you put it like that, yea," Joe replied.

"Dantwan!" Tyson shouted waiting a reply of agreement.

"Damn right I do! You'n even have to ask me at all, man" Dantwan agreed.

"Well brotha's let's go to work. It's going to be a long night." Tyson informed his crew shoving a pile of money in front of Joey and Dantwan.

They began counting the money at 8:30 that night and didn't finish until 3:45 the next morning. They split the money three ways, totaling three hundred-sixty thousand dollars, a piece.

"Well boys, I believe it's time to close up shop and go home to our wives." Tyson yawned, placing his hand over his mouth.

"I do believe that you're right Ty." Joey agreed.

"What about the coke?" Dantwan asked.

"We will handle that tomorrow night." Ty replied standing up to stretch his legs.

"That's cool with me." Joey agreed.

"I'm with that move too." Dantwan agreed standing up from the table.

"Listen up. Don't go around spending money like y'all crazy because we gotta let this shit blow over, plus they might be watching us." Tyson stated with a serious look on his face, meaning every word he said.

"Whatever." Dantwan replied.

"Dantwan, listen man, low-key for real, aight." Tyson shouted.

"Damn man you taking shit too serious. I feel you dog. I was just fucking with you man, loosen up a little." Dantwan back paddled, all while thinking of ways to spend his money.

"Ty drop me off at my girl house." Joey stated.

"Drop me off at the block." Dantwan stated.

"Really Dantwan, drop you off on the hot block with all that money on you?" Tyson stated sarcastically knowing Dantwan was on some bullshit. "Well aight to the hood then, nigga."

They all walked out of the door of the one-bedroom shack house, leaving the trash bags full of coke behind. Joey had his share of money ducked taped to his body while Tyson had his share in a backpack. Dantwan tucked his share into his shirt and pants looking like he had gained a hundred pounds.

Tyson drove to the hood called, *Fieldcrest* apartments a.k.a *Brick City* now the reformed Jesse Jackson Town homes. Tyson pulled up three doors down from Joey's girlfriend, Jackie Tucker's apartment to let him out.

Jackie was considered a ghetto hood rat, age 25 with no promising future. Fieldcrest at this time was one of the most dangerous neighborhoods in Greenville, South Carolina. If it wasn't a gunfight going down between two rival gangs then it was the jump out boys raiding and kicking in some poor hustlers apartment door. Jackie had three children that lived with her. Two of the children were boys named Brian, the oldest and Eric, the youngest. The little girl's name was Lorey which was her sister's daughter. Both of Jackie's boys were also by two different men. However, Lorey and Eric shared the same father. All day and all night long, Jackie kept young hustlers on her front porch selling drugs, drinking malt liquor, smoking marijuana, and playing with loaded guns.

Jackie never once considered getting her and her children out of Fieldcrest, she just figured that this is what life had to offer her and she was going to make the best of it.

Jackie was not a bad looking girl in fact she was cute as a belly button, but the way she carried herself and dressed made her look trashy inside and out. Jackie had a body like the singer, Beyonce. She had short hair which she always kept a weave hair due, to make up the difference. Jackie was also known as the drama queen around town, stayed into some shit. She stayed getting into arguments and fights about bullshit. Whenever she went out to the club, party, or cookout, or any type of gathering, please believe that she would end up in a fight.

When Joey and Jackie first met she was nothing like the drama queen she is now. It was over a matter of time when the real Jackie came out and it was too late for Joey to abandon ship. She had already sunk her claws into him and like my grandma would say, Joey loved her dirty draws.

- - - - -

Joey went behind one of the apartment buildings as quickly as possible, trying not to be seen with money ducked taped to his body. He knew that one slip up and he would become a victim of a sweet lick. He also knew that some of the guys in *Brick City* didn't like him. Being known for selling the best dope, getting all the clientele doesn't leave a good taste in other mothafucka's mouths. If it wasn't for some of the most respected, older hard hitters protecting him, he would have been 6 feet under by now. The old timers took to Joey because he was smart and stayed in school when all of us dropped out. He even graduated and that earned him respect and protection. I guess the hard hitters lived vicariously through him wishing they had chosen a different path in life. At any rate, Joey was off limits and nobody touched him.

As he walked around the apartment building he was greeted by a crackhead named Reader Tucker, Jackie's older sister, who hardly many people knew. Nobody knew the secret between Jackie and Reader, not even Joey, but every 1st of the month Jackie would snatch poor little Reader up by her collar and take her welfare check. One time Joey had to pull Jackie off Reader because Reader tried to hide from Jackie to avoid giving up her check.

"What's up Red you holding?" Reader whispered.

"Nah ain' holding nothing right now." Joey replied while peeping his surroundings to make sure no one is lurking.

"You know them blues been around here all day. They ran up in Ricky Mack girlfriend's apartment. They found a baby eight and a Glock 40 and took her straight to jail"

"For real." Joey asked still checking blind spots for anybody lurking.

"Yea man and them young dumbass boys up the street robbed the corner store again. Reader told like a snitch being interrogated under bright lights. This their third time robbing the same damn store."

Yea these young dudes stupid as hell. Well let me get in this house girl. Joey started walking off towards the door.

Joe, you think you can spot a bitch ten dollars?" Reader asked, trying to get money for her next hit.

First things first, stop referring to yourself as a bitch but check this out, tomorrow I'mma swing through and bless you, and your goal is to make *it*, make money for you, aight? He took his last look at Reader for the night thinking about how beautiful she used to be before she got addicted to that Snow White.

"Ok baby boy, I'll holla at you tomorrow then." She said as she disappeared into the dark alley.

Joey walked into Jackie's apartment through the back door. He hit the light switch on the side of the wall next to the door. He stood briefly watching the roaches break for cover. Sitting in the corner was a rat trap with peanut butter, cheese ,and a shaking rat with blood running down it's neck.

Joey was too tired to clean up the mess. He sat down at the kitchen table shaking head as his eyes went from the rat trap to the empty malt liquor bottles, loose cigar wrappers, and tobacco spread out on the table. He eyed the dirty dishes stacked in the sink, the counter tops, and stove.

"This shit don't make no sense at all."

He went to the refrigerator for a cold beer to only find a big jug of cold water, an old box of Arm & Hammer baking soda, and some small roaches living their best life, staying cool.

"Damn this some nasty shit."

Joey plopped back down in the chair he just emerged from. He flashed back to seeing his best friend Chris fall to his death.

*All we was trying to do was make a quick come up so we could get away from this life.* He thought about the 1st day he meet Chris in the   fifth grade at Lake Forest Elementary School.

Joey and Chris was dating the same girl. Can't really call it dating in the fifth grade but you couldn't tell them that. One day on the playground they got into a fight over the girl. The fight lasted longer than either of them wanted it to. Both the boys were glad when the fight was broken up. But not before Joey landed the last punch to Chris's jaw in victory.

Funny thing is after the fight the girl that they were fighting over decided that she didn't want nothing to do with either of them. Come to find out she was seeing fat Willie Yeargin on the side. Heated and vengeful Chris and Joey took turns slapping the girl around for humiliating them. It was then that Chris and Joey became the best of friends, tight as twin brothers.

Joey jumped as he was startled by a roach crawling on his arm. *Damn*! He yelled so loud it caused Jackie to wake up, trailing downstairs to investigate.

She stood with her hands on her hips at the entrance of the kitchen. "Where the fuck you been?" Standing half drunk and blunted out.

"Look, I don't want to hear that shit tonight Jackie." Joey called her by her first name instead of the usual boo, babygirl, or suga to let her know he meant what he said.

"I don't give a fuck what you don't want to hear. You don't be coming up in my shit all time of night like you run my shit!" Jackie spat back as if she actually established rules and regulations that was actually followed.

"Would you please shut the fuck up bitch!"

"Oh no you didn't call me a bitch!" She yelled, while waving her hands in the air and waiting on Joey to retract what he said.

"Listen Jackie, I'm tired and I got a lot on my mind tonight, so would you please fall the fuck back." He said as calmly as he could.

"What bitch is on your mind?" She smacked her teeth, waiting on a reply.

"Hear we go with this shit." Joey mumbled, but Jackie heard him loud and clear.

"Damn right, here we go." Jackie stated, sucking her teeth and rolling her eyes and neck with her hands placed on the back on her hip, leaning against the wall staring at Joey.

"Fuck this shit! I'm outta here. He rose out of the chair and dotted towards the back door.

"Leave mothafucka and don't come back." She followed Joey to the back door then slammed it behind him. She posted up for a few minutes to make sure he wouldn't change his mind. A few minutes passed by so she began walking up the stairs to her bedroom. She plopped down on the bed before yelling, "You can come out the damn closet boy, he's gone!"

"You sure that nigga gone?" Lendon asked with his pants and boxers down to his knees.

"Yeah nigga, now finish beating this pussy up." Jackie said while lying back on the bed, folding her legs behind her neck.

Even though Lendon was a little nervous, what nigga bout to turn down some wet ass pussy cause a nigga popped up. "You made sure to lock that door back?"

"Boy gimme that dick and stop playing, ain't no rookie."

Lendon did just that. He shook off the nerves, beat it up and cuddled with Jackie until morning.

- - - - -

Joey walked through the streets paranoid as hell with all that cash duck taped to his body. He looked at every bush, tree, and dark alley to see who might be lurking ready to ambush him. He watched the all nighters, (crackheads and dealers) running and chasing cars to either to buy dope or sell dope.

He spotted Reader standing by a grey Ford truck talking to the driver through the passenger side window. He didn't see any other passengers, so he yelled out for her.

"Yo Reader!" He stood about ten feet away. And she lifted her head towards his direction.

"Yeah, what's up Red? I thought you were in for the night."

"Couldn't sleep."

"Yeah right. That crazy bitch went off on you again, didn't she? She just don't know when to keep her mouth and legs closed do she?" But Joey didn't catch the hint she gave him.

"You know her better than I do?" He said while looking into the car to peep the driver. Is you people in the car cool? He nodded towards the driver.

"They're trying to cop something, you working?"

"Tell him I'll give him ten dollars to run me across town."

"What you gone to do for me?" Reader, chronic for a hit.

"I got you baby girl." Joey said with a glimpse of longing in his eyes, wishing that she wasn't a crackhead because he would surely make her his.

Reader immediately got the driver to agree to make a quick dash across town. Joey got into the truck, once positioned in the seat, he handed Reader a twenty-dollar bill. Satisfied Reader walked off with her come up for the night.

"Stop by the Citgo first then dash across town, aight."

# CHAPTER 2

After Tyson and Dantwan dropped Joey off in Fieldcrest, they headed towards Nicholtown Community, where they were born and raised. Tyson didn't hang on this side of town anymore but Joey and Dantwan hung there faithfully and knew everybody who was somebody, coming and going.

"Stop right here and let me out on Rebecca street by Phillie Red Club- Delisas." Dantwan ordered.

They spotted three third shift dealers posted up near the club's entrance.

"Who them niggas' in front of the club?"

"It looks like Fat Mama and John John." Dantwan replied opening the car door.

"Aye you sure you wanna get out here with all that money on you?"

"Ain't no nigga gone rob me Ty. Dantwan replied like he's immune from getting jacked.

"Wouldn't it be best to go put the money up first or do you want me to hold it to be on the safe side, man?"

Tyson didn't agree with Dantwan's decision to get out of the car with all that money on him. Because as soon as one of them fuck boys get in their heads, it's money or dope and feeling cocky, they taking that shit.

"Nigga I got this, you handle yours and I'll handle mine, aight? Dantwan snapped back, closing the car door behind him.

Tyson put his 1988 GT Escort into drive but before he put his foot on the gas he looked out his rear view mirror at Dantwan walking towards the club where the guys were still standing outside. To his surprise Dantwan walked past the club.

*Good.* Tyson was relieved, knowing exactly where Dantwan was headed.

Before Dantwan made it to the next block he heard someone calling his name in a low whisper.

"Aye Dantwan."

Dantwan grabbed his Glock nine from his waist band, looking around for the suspect. He eased his figure on the trigger and pointed as he saw movement and a dark figure walking towards him.

"Who dat is?" Dantwan called out.

"A.J. nigga and stop pointing that gun."

"Oh shit! My nigga what's poppin' around here playboy?" Dantwan replied excited to see his main man.

"It's mad slow out here tonight. I haven't made nothing but a hundred and twenty dollars.

"How long you gonna be out here? Dantwan asked looking around and checking his surroundings.

Why?"

"Cause it's gone to take me about fifteen minutes to go pull this lick and I'll be right back." Dantwan said, as he tried to step away in the direction he was originally headed.

Anxious to join in on the lick, "Let me go."

"Nah man wait right here I'll be back." Dantwan said, as he began walking down the dark street.

"That's fucked up Dantwan. We supposed to be road dawgs." A.J. scuffed at Dantwan.

Just wait right there and when I come back we gon' ball til we fall.

"Don't have me waiting here for nothing nigga and hurry back.

Dantwan disappeared around the corner. He picked up his pace and started jogging. About 3 minutes later he was jumping a fence to his mother's back yard.

He headed to the garage and stood there for a minute with his hands on his knees catching his breath. Once he caught his breath he began pulling the money out of his shirt and pants. He counted 10 stacks and stuffed it into his front pockets. He took a hundred thousand and crawled up the garage wall with the help of a large workbench and remove a loose panel. Then stuffed the hundred thousand into the hole as far back as he could reach. Once he replaced the board he wiped off the spider webs and dust from his clothes.

He walked out of the garage and headed towards the back of the house. He crawled under the house and began digging a hole about 2ft deep to hide two hundred thousand dollars before existing the crawl space into his moms house. No lights were on except a small lamp in the front room, that always remained on at night. The light reflection allowed Dantwan to move throughout the house without knocking anything over. Once entering his room he hid another 50 grand in a shoebox under his bed for easy access.

*I'mma bless my moms and few other people with this right here.* Feeling blessed that he has the opportunity to do a good deed.

After hiding the money, Dantwan began running back to meet up with A.J.. Dantwan was back in Nicoletown near the club in no time. He spotted A.J. making a quick sale.

"What's up nigga?" Smiling showing a mouth full of gold fronts.

"What took you so long, I was about to jet on your ass." A.J. laughed.

"Business nigga."

"Nigga you ain't got no business." A.J. smiled back at Dantwan.

"Fuck that shit, lets get out of here." Dantwan started walking east towards Roosevelt apartments.

A.J.pulled out a half ounce of weed and a swisher sweet cigar from the pocket of his windbreaker. The two men stepped off the side walk into a wooded area behind the apartments as A.J finished rolling his blunt. He took a puffed then passed it to Dantwan.

"Ain't shit to get into." Dantwan said, as he reached for the blunt.

"Old girl came through today looking for you." A.J told Dantwan in-between coughs.

"Who? Tammy?"

"Hell no nigga, your stalker."

"Man that's not my girl, that bitch be following a nigga around and shit. I ain't even put this meat shank in her yet." They both began laughing.

"Yeah right nigga."

"For real dog, I haven't hit that."

"Yo Dee, Lisa is not a bad looking girl plus she got a banging body. It's better than Tammy high yellow ass."

"Facts."

A.J. and Dantwan sat in the wooded area getting high for another 10 minutes, bored out of their minds.

"Fuck it lets go down to her apartment." Dantwan suggested.

"Who's apartment?"

"To crazy Lisa's apartment." They began laughing again.

"You gone hit that aint'cha?" Thinking about how thick Lisa is.

"I'm going to beat her back out. Man let's bounce. She got her cute ass cousin staying with her too."

"Prospect huh?"

"Yep."

"Aight. I'm game."

They rose from the oak stumps they were sitting on and began walking down the trail along the back of the apartments. Dantwan couldn't help but think about putting Lisa in the buck and hoping his homeboy get a taste of her little cousin. As they entered the breeze way they saw a few guys standing out front , Wild Irish Rose and Budweisers. Not wanting to draw attention to themselves, Dantwan and A.J. speed up and continued to walk towards the apartment.

# CHAPTER 3

"After we leave the Citgo Station buddy, where too?" The driver named Steve, asked.

"Just drive and I'll tell you when we get to that point." The driver agreed, putting petal to the metal. They engaged in small talk on the way. Joey didn't want to share any information with Steve and was glad that Steve was all about the money and nothing more.

Seven minutes later they arrived at the gas station and front of the gas pump. As Joey got out of the car he ducked his head back inside the truck.

"Hey partner, you want something?"

"Yea let me get a Bull and a pack of Newports."

Joey walked towards the double doors of the gas station and immediately headed towards the back of the store to gather a twelve pack of Coors light extra gold, a Bull, a pint of Mad Dog 20/20 and grabbed a bag of Taki's on the way to the register.

"That will be $15.63, Sir." A soft delicate voice spoke, but Joey didn't raise his head to see the beauty before him.

"Add a box of Black and Milds and two packs of Newports with that please." Joey ordered, with his head down pulling money out of his pocket.

"Will you be paying for the gas too"

"Sure go ahead."

"That'll be $38.16."

Making eye contact, he was stunned by her beauty, he handed her a fifty dollar bill. "Cool baby girl, keep the change."

He began walking out of the store but stopped and turned around,

"Excuse me miss, can I ask you a question?" He smiled, showing all of his pretty pearly white teeth.

"Sure shoot."

He paused for a few seconds to gaze into her brown eyes and Mexican pecan brown skin.

"Why does your man let you work late hours in a convenient store, in this drug infested neighborhood?"

"I don't have a man. Bills and school cost a lot so I gotta do what I gotta do." She replied, as she stacked a fresh carton of New Ports.

"I feel you. Well let me ask you another question." Joey replied, walking back towards the counter.

"Customers these days sure do ask a lot of questions." She responded, looking Joey up and down checking out his swag.

"Wouldn't that be better than complaints." He replied, showing his pearly white smile again, "For real though, what's your name?"

"Paula." She smiled ear to ear.

"Nice to meet you Paula, my name is Joey." He smiled ear to ear, showing those pearly whites again.

"Nice to meet you too, Joey but customers are coming in so I have to get back to work."

Can I call you sometime, maybe take you out for dinner, so we can get further acquainted?"

"I tell you what, call the store then we can see if we can make plans."

By this time two girls entered the store and made their way to the counter with a twelve pack of Coolers. One of the girls stood next to Joey looking him up and down checking his swag while the other girl placed the content on the counter.

Paula motioned for Joey to come to the counter. She quickly grabbed Joey's hand and wrote the store number on his palm enclosed in a heart.

"Don't loose it." She smiled.

"Oh I won't." He smiled back as he walked backwards towards the exit.

- - - - -

Tyson pulled into his yard in his 1988 GT Escort next to a red Honda Accord and parked. When Tyson stepped out of his car he heard his dogs coming full speed from the back of his two bedroom house. As he watched the two big black spots leap in the air towards him, Tyson yelled, *Nooo* and began laughing as his twin retrievers jumped all over him with muddy paws.

Man and Minnie were his two furry friends, all black with white spots in the middle of their chests. As the dogs played and licked him, he wondered why they were not chained. He brushed it off figuring, Tonya finally took his advise and let them roam free.

"Alright get down." Tyson barked while laughing and asking if they were hungry in his dog voice. The dogs began to bark then suddenly the porch lights came on and a small sleepy voice spoke.

"Baby is that you?" Tonya asked sticking her head out of the side door as she held a 38 special with the hammer, cocked and ready to shoot.

"Yeah it's me baby." I'll be in in a minute. He led the dogs to the back of the house to lock them up and fed them.

"Make it quick baby." Tonya had been waiting and worrying about him all night.

"Alright I'm just gonna feed them real quick." He poured dog food in their bowls as quickly as he could.

Before entering the house he dusted his feet off on the doormat. He entered the kitchen and saw a warm plate sitting on the stove with a note on it. As he read the note, Tonya walked into the kitchen.

"How was your day baby?" She asked as she walked towards the refrigerator retrieving a carton of orange juice.

"Rough."

"What's wrong baby?" She asked as she stepped behind him rubbing his chest.

"I'm just tired, I guess." Not really wanting to tell Tonya about his day.

Well come lay your head on mommies lap and tell me all about it. She started walking towards the living room couch signaling for him to come join her.

Tyson grabbed the Orange juice carton and took a gulp before heading to the couch. He laid his head on her lap. They enjoyed each others company in complete silence. And Tyson drifted off in space thinking about how much he loves Tonya. She's the best decision he's ever made.

Tyson and Tonya had been living together for three years but have dated for five years. They met at a car show in Greenwood SC. When he first saw her he knew that she was trying to catch a big time baller from the way she dressed and carried herself. Although Tyson was dabbling in the street life he was not a big time hustler and didn't have big time money. He just assumed she saw the potential in him and never once thought he wasn't good enough.

Tyson was dabbling in the street lift, getting a little paper here and there but he wasn't a drug dealer. In fact, his trade was jacking the drug dealers, and it wasn't until the recent lick that he involved other people.

Tonya saw that potential in Tyson and knew that one day he would get major money that will set them up for life. So she held on tight to her ticket out of the projects and into luxury.   But somewhere along the way she fell in love with Tyson and didn't care if he got rich or not. She was going to ride with him to hell and back if she had to. Tyson laid his head on Tonya's lap and fell asleep while Tonya held his head.

- - - - -

Joey exited the store, walking back to the truck to find Steve rambling around in the back seat.

Joey looked into the car, "Whats up partner?" Trying to see what the driver was looking for.

"Man I'm looking for my beer cup." Pulling his beer cup from under the seat.

"You stay prepared don't you?" Laughing as he took one last glance at Paula through the glass windows.

"These days you have to." Steve stated as he put the key back into the ignition.

"You know where Nichole Town is right?" Joey closed, the door after hopping in the front seat, placing the bag of beer between his legs. He pulled out a Bull and handed it to the Steve.

"Sure." Steve replied, cracking open the beer and poured it into his cup. He pulled off and took a back road to Nicoletown. Ten minutes later they arrived on Rebecca Street and made a right turn on Elder Street.

"Right here, the green house." Joey pointed for the driver to stop as he gathered his things. He opened the car door to excite.

"Guess I'll see you around young man."

"Aight."

The driver pulled off as Joey yelled. "YOOO!" The driver stopped and back up.

"I forgot to pay you." Joey handed Steve a 20 dollar bill.

"I'm good partner, you put ten in the tank."

"Nah, take this anyway." Joey insisted as he shoved the 20 dollars in Steve's hand.

The driver took the money and drove off. Joey waited until the driver disappeared before he began moving. He went around the back of the abandoned house and jumped the fence. Before walking three blocks to Sunset drive to a two bedroom yellow house with flowers landscaped through the yard.

The sun was now rising as little kids with backpacks strolled to their designated bus stops. He heard some of the boys cracking jokes on each other. He let out a giggle, boy I remember those days when me and Chris would crack jokes on each other and the little girls. The little girls would always swing on us and we would use it as an excuse to grab a little butt in the process.

Joey opened the back door, entering the kitchen to find his grandmother up at the crack of dawn doing what she alway does. After all these years, since her husband and daughter passed away, she still gets up every morning to cook a big breakfast.

Joey walked to his grandmother and kissed her on the cheek, "Grandma, why you cooking all that food?"

"We gotta eat don't we."

"Yeh I suppose so." He smirked as she smiled back.

Joey walked to his room where he spent most of his childhood years. He placed the bag of beer on the floor and unstrapped the money from his body. He retrieved a brown leather back pack from under his bed and put the money inside it, then placed it back under his bed until he could think of a better hiding place.

He tossed his body on his bed exhausted. His head bounced on his soft fluffy pillow as he fell fast to sleep.

# CHAPTER 4

The sun was nearing as Dantwan and A.J. stood at Lisa's front door. Dantwan reached into his pocket and pulled out a thousand dollars and handed it to A.J.

"Put this in your pocket, Thats you my nigga." Smiling at A.J.

"Word!" A.J.'s eyes stretch from excitement.

"That's nothing dog, you my main man. I got something else for you later on. Dantwan boasted feeling good that he could look out for his people.

Dantwan knocked on Lisa's screen door. They could see through the apartment because the door was open. A Little girl made her way to the door. Dressed in daisy dukes with a durag on her head and a pair of pink vans. The girl looked at Datwan then to A.J.,

"Who is you?"

"Dantwan"

The girl who looked every bit of sixteen but was twenty-one rushed through the apartment without letting them in screaming Lisa's name. Thirty-seconds later Lisa and the young girl returned to the door.

"What's poppin Lisa?" Dantwan asked smiling revealing his gold fronts.

Although Lisa had butterflies in her belly and wanted to jump Dantwan bones right there in the door way she kept her composure and whispered in a pouty voice.

"Boy I got company."

"See what I'm talking about, soon as I want to give you a chance with *Big Dee,* you choose another nigga over me. That's why I don't fuck with you now." Laying it on thick knowing Lisa wanted him and would do anything to have him.

"I'm sorry." Lisa whispered.

"Don't never be sorry, kick that busta ass nigga up out your shit."

"I can't do that."

"Fuck it then I'm out and don't fuck with me when you see me trick."

Lisa's cousin Karen put her two cents in,

"Fuck that nigga you don't need him." Rolling her eyes and sucking her teeth.

Lisa then weighed her options and thought about how long she's been chasing Dantwan to finally be at this moment.

"Hold up Dantwan, don't go nowhere." Dantwan playfully punched A.J. in the arm as Lisa disappeared into the apartment approaching Tony and his homeboy Mike. They had been drinking and smoking weed for a little over 3 hours before Dantwan and A.J. interrupted.

Lisa let them know that they had to leave. Of course Tony was disappointed because just like Datwan, Tony wanted to get into Lisa guts too.

"That's fucked up girl and you know it." Karen stated pissed

20

that Lisa was kicking the men out. She took to Mike like rice cause he spent money on them and promised to take her to out to dinner later.

"I don't want to hear that shit. You can leave with them if you want to." Lisa snapped back.

Karen walked off to the back bedroom pissed off.

"Ok y'all got to go." Lisa demanded.

"Bro this fucked up." Tony said as he and Mike got up from the couch and Lisa walked them to the door.

As the two emerged, Datwan and A.J. stood leaning on the wall waiting to be welcomed in. Tony and Mike looked Dantwan and A.J. up and down like they had something to say. Dantwan and A.J. laughed in amusement.

"You find something funny nigga?" Tony asked.

"Yeah nigga them tight as pants you got on, nigga." Dantwan spat back as A.J. laughed harder.

"Come on Tony man we aint looking for trouble over no bitches." Mike encouraged.

"Yeah take ya partner's advice nigga. You aint getting no pussy here tonight. A.J. laughed while holding his 25 automatic in his jacket letting them know he's got it and ready.

The two headed down the stairs to an Infinity sitting on 24's. They got in the truck and started the engine. As they pulled off 2-Pac's, "Ambition of a Rider" bumped from the speakers which could be heard two blocks away. Once the truck disappeared Dantwan closed the door behind them.

As Tony and Mike drove up the street to Roosavelt apartments they came to the red light. Tony made a right turn thinking to himself how he just got played and it didn't sit well with him.

" Yo Mike you how them nigga's tried to play us?"

"Tried my ass them niggas played the fuck outta us."

Tony saw one of his dope fiends flagging him down. So he pulled over to the curve on Rebecca Street.

"Imma have to get at them niggas for that disrespectful shit, bro." Tony said as he rolled down the window to retrieve 35 dollars in exchange for 2 rocks.

"Man fuck them niggas and bitches." We are trying to get this money bro." Mike replied bobbing his head to the music.

"True." Tony made a mental note that he would run into them niggas again and handle his shit.


Inside Lisa apartment it was flushed from top to bottom. She had wall to wall beige carpet with a brown leather matching couch set, lazy boy recliner and loveseat. A 62 inch big screen tv hanging on the wall. Gold curtains veering the windows and matching lamps on the end tables. A painting of some sort of African artwork hung throughout the living room and down the hall as far as he could see.

"Lisa what's your cousin name?"

"Karen."

"I can talk for myself, I'm not mute or nothing." Karen yelled from the kitchen still feeling a little salty about Mike having to leave.

"Well girl what's your name since you can talk for yourself."

Karen walked into the living room sucking her teeth.

"My name, Karen."

"Another Nutty Buddy A.J." Dan,twan laughed.

"Nigga grow up off that shit down grading me and shit."

"My bad baby girl come on over here and sit on daddys' lap." Lisa damn near broke her neck trying to get to Dantwan's lap.

"A shorty y'all smoke?" A.J. tried getting Karen to relax and open up to him but she snapped back.

"The name is Karen not shorty."

"Why so hostile Karen, we just came to chill and have a good time. You want to have a good time don't you?" Dantwan chimed in.

"Nah nigga ya'll think y'all getting some pussy. Karen spat back rolling her eyes and sucking her teeth.

Datwan and A.J. started laughing because she was right.

"Karen, let me talk to you." Lisa headed towards her bedroom as Karen followed. They both sat down on the edge of Lisa's king size bed covered in bears and throw pillows with red satin sheets and a red comforter.

"Look Karen I know you don't know them niggas but I love Dantwan and I've been trying to get him to settled down with me since the first day I laid eyes on him. So please, please don't fuck this up for me girl."

"Aight big cuz but if that otha nigga thinking he's going to get some pussy for free he's got another thing coming."

"Look I'll give you a hundred dollars when I get paid if you just go with the flow." Lisa replied sounding desperate.

"Aight I'm game cuz." Karen said as she got off the bed and walked over to the mirror to make sure she was looking her best, seeing dollar signs in her eyes.

"Bitch that's all it took, hoe."

"It takes a ho to know one." They both laughed.


Meanwhile Dantwan and A.J. had a discussion of their own. They had decided they wanted to switch the game and take pussy off the table. They wanted to chill, smoke weed, and get to know the ladies.

Lisa and Karen came out of the room laughing. Lisa headed right to Dantwan's lap while Karen plopped down on the love seat next to A.J. giving him her attention.

"Damn, Karen change of attitude huh?" Dantwan stated.

"Leave her alone and worry about what's sitting on your lap." Lisa stated grabbing Dantwan's chin, turning his head towards her.

"That's right boy mind your own business." Karen snapped.

"She still haven't lost that slick mouth though." A. J. added.

"It's mine." Karen responded smirking at A.J. who tried to reach for her thighs to squeeze it but Karen quickly moved her leg," Gotta be quicker than that." She laughed.

"Oh shit I almost forgot I have to be at work in an hour. Time moving too fast." Lisa looked at her watch, showing its 5 am.

"Call your job and tell them you won't be in today." Dantwan demanded.

"Nigga is you crazy?" Lisa rose from Dantwan's lap as her entire life depended on her job.

Dantwan pulled that famous move. "How much you make a day?"

"I make 10 an hour so that's a 100 a day."

"Make the phone call, I'll double your whole paycheck right

now."

"Stop lying boy."

Dantwan reached into his pockets to prove his word could be trusted.

"You must want some pussy bad." Lisa laughed.

"Nah I just want to chill and get to know you better. That's what you been wanting from me, right?" Dantwan showed a glimpse of his vulnerable side.

"I guess there's hope after all."Karen chimed in shocked to hear Dantwan talking vulnerable like that.

"Fuck what he's talking about I want some pussy." A.J. laughed.

"Well that hope just went down the drain and I stand corrected. Y'all mofo just want to fuck." Karen sucked her teeth.

"Damn shortie, can't you take a joke. You take shit too seriously." A.J. mean mugged her.

"Boy if I have to tell you one more time that my name is Karen not shortie. We gone have a problem."

"And my name is A.J. not boy. He snapped back.

Lisa made a phone call to her job and requested a day off her usual 9 to 5 manufacturing job which wasn't a big deal. They kept different temp services on speed dial and could get someone in to cover her shift within the hour. All her boss said was to make sure she returned on Monday because they had a big order to fill.

They all commenced to drinking a bottle of Paul Mason, watching tv and smoking weed. An hour later Karen and A.J. were passed out drunk on the floor while Lisa laid in Dantwan's arms with a smile on her face as they slept on the couch until 3P.M. that afternoon.

# CHAPTER 5

Tyson was awakened out of his snoring by his phone ringing. He jumped up from the couch while answering his phone and checking the time. *Damn its 8 o'clock in the morning already.*

"Yeah tell it," Tyson answered with sleep in his eyes.

"What's good my nigga?"

Tyson heard an unfamiliar voice, "Who is this?"

"Ray Ray nigga, damn!"

"Oh yeah what's happening?"

"We need to talk asap."

"Where?"

"Where the eagles lay their eggs." Ray Ray suggested.

"Nah." Never trusting no one Tyson changed the location. "Where the bears take their shit, 8:15 sharp." Tyson knew he could reach this location in 10 minutes flat.

"Impossible." Ray Ray replied thinking about how fast he would have to push his car to reach the location in time.

"Well we must don't need to talk, do we?" Tyson replied with a smile.

"Aight I'll be there."

Tyson walked into his bedroom where Tonya laid in bed watching one of her favorite talk shows.

Tonya looked up with a smile on her face. "Good morning baby." Moving the covers back so he could join her.

"Not right now baby, I'll right back. I have to handle some business. Tyson reached in the closet grabbing his windbreaker.

"Where you going?" She asked even though he told her several times not to ask him where he's going.

"Business baby." Tyson walked towards the bedroom door to leave the house.

"Be careful." She pulled the covers back over her body.

The words, Be Careful, put a sour taste in Tyson's mouth. He hated when she told him that. He always felt it jinx a nigga in the game. But he tried to be patient with her this morning.

"Alright." He yelled back trying to get out of the house.

"Hold up Ty."

"What!"

"Give me a kiss before you leave."

Tyson rushed to the bedroom and pecked her on the lips then made a dash for the front door.

Tyson scurried three houses down. Opened the 3 car garage and hopped on black mimi bike while putting the helmet on his head. Before putting metal to the pedal.

He pulled into the law firm parking lot at the same time Ray Ray did, and watched him park his brand new Benz.

As Ray Ray got out his car he checked his surroundings looking for Tyson. He had never seen Tyson motorcycle so he was looking for the black crown vic with rims.

Tyson pulled in front of him and stopped. Glanced out Ray's clothes and even though he had on a silk shirt and slack with gator boots, demanded, "Get on."

Ray go on the back holding scared to death as Tyson pushed the bike fast. He went down back roads and came out on a small street which led to Timothy's park off highway 25, that has gotten a bad name due to quite a few killings there.

Tyson parked the bike as they got off he motioned Tay to follow him. They ended up in a wooded area down a narrow path. Tyson stopped in a secluded section of the woods where they could not be seen but could see everything.

"What's going on partner?" Tyson wanted to get straight to the point.

"Of course you already know the heat is on." Ray Ray looked at Tyson like he fucked up on the robbery.

"How hot?" Tyson asked.

"Texas Pete hot. What was you thinking about? The lick was to go clean. Nobody was suppose to get shot, let alone killed." Ray Ray questioned.

"Have anybody contacted you yet?" Tyson studied Ray's face for the truth or a lie.

"Two of their goons showed up at my spot this morning. Beating my fucking door down.

"What did you tell them?

"I didn't tell them shit." I got the fuck up out of their through the side window and left them mothafucka's beating down my front and back door.

"Good who else know about this lic'?"

"Just me, you and your team."

"Man you trying to set me up?" Tyson stepped closer to Ray and looked him eye to eye.

"What the fuck you talking about nigga, you high or something?" Ray tensed up.

"Then who the fuck is that man over there. He has been following us since we met up. Ray turned to look into the direction Tyson pointed in as Tyson reached around Ray's neck with a Rambo knife and slid it across his juggler, crushing his wind pipe all in one swift motion.

Tyson laid Ray's shaking body down, slowly on the ground and watched him take his last breath. Tyson placed his hands over Ray's eyes to close his eyelids before dragging his body deeper in the wooded area by his feet. He placed leaves and scrub branches over his body to cover him up.

Tyson went back to his bike relieved that no witnesses were around to take care of and he no longer had Ray panicking over his shoulders. He hopped back on his bike putting his helmet on and drove back to his house. His Safe Haven that nobody knew about. He parked his bike and went inside. He stripped off his clothes and tossed them into the fireplace. He pressed a button on the side of the wall next to the fireplace and flames emerged causing a roaring fire. He watched his clothes burn down to ashes before going to his closet to retrieve his blue sweat suit to change into. He set the alarm and locked the door as he left to go three houses down where he rested his head at night with his lady.

Tonya met him at the door with Man and Ming standing beside her with tears in her eyes.

"Ms. Hill called while you were gone."

"What Chris done did now?"

"Chris is dead," Tonya cried out.

"What!" Tyson put on a 5 star performance. I'll be right back!"

"Not without me, I'm going too." She demanded while wrapping her arms around Tyson, laying her head in his chest.

They grabbed a couple of items and got into her red Honda Accord to head to Nicholtown where Chris's mother lived. When they pulled up, there were family, friends, and people who just wanted to be nosey surrounding the house. Tyson jumped out of the car before it was at a full stop and rushed over to Ms. Hill.

"How you holding up Ms. Hill, he asked as he hugged her tightly in his arms.

"I'm going to be ok baby, I'll be alright." Ms. Hill said, as tears rolled down her cheeks while holding Tyson just as tight.

"How are you holding up Joey?" Tyson asked his friend, who stood within arms reach behind Ms. Hill.

"I just got the news ten minutes ago and rushed straight over here."

Tyson looked around at the crowd surrounding the house.

"Can somebody please tell me what the fuck is going on? Who did this! Huh! Somebody better tell me something! Spread the word I'm coming for whoever did it!"

Tonya reached out for Tyson, Watch your mouth baby in front of Ms. Hill."

"That's alright baby, I understand what he's going through."

31

Tyson turned to Ms. Hill still yelling, "I will get to the bottom of this and somebody is gonna pay." Bringing more attention to himself, not knowing that in the midst of the crowd stood Detective Hoffman of homicide, talking and taking statements from anybody who would talk.

"Somebody is going to pay for this." Detective Hoffman directed his attention to Tyson. "Don't go getting ahead of yourself young man. The police will handle this matter. Don't you think 2 murders is enough already."

"Two!" Joey asked.

"Well two bodies were found burned at the scene of crime. One identified as Chris Hill and the other of Pedro Gormez, a well known drug dealer in Greenville. But until we complete a proper investigation that's all the information I can provide.

"So when can we expect to hear something?"

"We will keep Ms. Hill informed as soon as we learn more information. Hoffman replied walking off towards his unmarked car.

- - - - -

Hoffman drove off thinking about the case trying to put together names and faces of suspects as his phone rung.

"Yeah."

"Have you found out anything yet?"

"No Sir but I am on a trail. I just left Chris Hill's house doing an investigation."

"Well keep me posted when you find something out."

"Will do Sir. Hoffman stated pulling into the Greenville County Police Station on 4 McGee Street.

# CHAPTER 6

Jesus Gormez sat behind his mahogany desk talking on the phone, making sure that Detective Hoffman understood the urgency of finding who killed his nephew. As Jesus turned his chair facing the window behind him he caught a glimpse of his slightly bald head and grey hair showing his age, and for a split second wondered how time has flown by then he heard a knock at his door.

Jesus weighing about two-hundred eighty pounds let out a heavy sigh as he glanced down at his Jacob's time piece wrapped around his wrist that could tell time in four different languages. He motioned for the two men to come in. They stood in front of his desk looking around the room that they've seen a million times, covered in cream carpet, bookshelves that lined the walls and the Mexican flag that was the first thing to catch anyone's attention.

As Jesus slammed the phone down, ending his call, he motioned for the two men to sit down.

"Tell me something good to brighten my day." He huffed.

"Mr. Gormez, Sir, we went by the spade Ray Ray's house this morning, He wasn't there. Julio Gormez, who is Jesus's second cousin.

"What do you mean nobody was there?" I have a nephew

murdered, one point two million missing in hard cash, two keys of raw heroin, and fifteen keys of uncut coke missing, plus my wive's period is on. And you're telling me that no one was home?" Why are you here!

"Sir I have talked with our contact at the police station and it has been discovered that another body was found in the fire. " Papi chimed in to ease Gormez's concerns about whether they'd been out doing their jobs.

"Do you have a name?"

"I believe it was Chris Hill, Sir." Papi reached inside of his pocket to retrieve a paper with the name written on it. Yes Sir, Chris Hill.

"I want to know everything about this Chris Hill. I want to know who his family is, who is friends are and who his enemies are. I want to know what was he doing in my stash house."

Jesus waived his hand to dismiss the men. Leave my office and don't come back until you have all his information, my money and my product. And fine Ray Ray and bring him to me immediately. I told him that if anything went wrong i would see to it myself that his balls be placed in a pig feet jar, now leave!" Gormez slammed his fist on his desk.

"Yes, Sir," The two men replied as they walked towards the door.

Jesus reached for the phone to call his niece.

"Sunshine."

"Good morning, Papi," Paula responded wiping the sleep out of her eyes.

"Wake up sleepy head." Jesus replied as he sat back in his chair loosening his tie. "We need to talk immediately."

"Papi I just got off work and laid down. I'm tired right now, can't it wait til later." Paula begged in a sweet soft voice.

"Get some sleep later this is very important. I will send a car for you immediately."

"Alright Papi, I'll be ready." Paula hung up the phone, let out a sigh and laid back down pulling the covers over her head screaming into her pillow. "Damn I just want to sleep!"

Twenty minutes later a black limousine with jet black tinted windows arrived at Paula's town house on the East side of Greenville, two miles away from Eastside high school. The bodyguard knocked for Paula.

"I'm coming." Still dragging her feet from no sleep and working all night.

Paula opened the door, walking past the bodyguard standing in her doorway. He watched her as she walked to the limo catching a glimpse of how nice her ass looked and jiggled in her sundress hoping to see skin as she bent over to slide in.

Paula and Pedro were first cousins. Pedro's father and Paula's mother were siblings. Paula's mother was Pauline Gormez. Pedro's father was Jesus's brother, Santana Gormez the 2nd. Both Paula and Pedro's parents were killed some years back in Mexico when the Gormez family went to war with the Gararo family over the underground turn pipes that were used to smuggle tons of heroin and cocaine into the United States. Also at this time their was a major drug drought when one of the most respected Cartels family business was infatuated by the United States special force during the Bill Clinton administration, a war on drugs encouraged by Hilary Clinton. After the deaths of Santana and Pauline Gormez, Jesus took Paula and Pedro into his home and they grew close as brothers and sisters.

Later as the story unfolds the real reason the two family's raged war was because Ricky Goraro slapped Megal Gormez, a high ranking member with a dangerous mean streak. And with that mean streak just three hours later had killed five of Ricka Gararo's men in broad daylight in front of a church temple after attending a Christening ceremony.

Ricka Gararo retaliated by ordering a hit of Megal and reported via an unknown source Megal's drug activity causing another raid. This raid captured over two thousands tons of cocaine and they burned 50 miles of marijuana fields. Causing Megal financial stability to crumble and forced him into hiding.

Megal contacted his last resource, another Cartel family who fronted him two tons of cocaine and five hundred keys of raw heroin to get back on his feet. Megal bounced back quick by lowballing his prices and taking full control of the turn pipe. Ricka's connects, soon came running to Megal for product causing Ricka to lose money.

Ricka soon called a meeting of truce with Megal and wanted to buy product at the same low price. However, Megal jacked up the price and sold Ricka some weak product. Ricka then summoned 20 Gararo men and sent them with explosives and weapons of choice to Megal's mini mansion.

They slaughtered everything in site including the cattle and horses. Pauline and Santana were also in the home. After the men slaughtered everything and everyone they blasted explosives in and outside the house. Ricka watched the blasts and flames with his binoculars from two hundred yards away. *Well done*!

- - - - -

Paula and the bodyguard arrived at Gormez's Ranch on Hardward Lake and excited the limo. They walked over to Gormez standing in the front door awaiting their arrival. Paula greeted her uncle with a big kiss on the cheek and tight hug.

"Follow me Sunshine." Gormez walked off the porch towards the open field. Paula followed quietly followed behind her uncle wondering what was so urgent that couldn't;t wait until she got proper beauty sleep. As Paula followed Down a wooded path they approached a filed surrounded by a long brown fence with horses galloping about.

Gormez stopped and turned, facing Paula.

"Sunshine I don't know how to tell you this, so I am going to be straight forward, Pedro is dead."

Paula's eyes began to fill with tears as her mouth dropped as her body became limp. Gormez quickly caught her before she hit the ground. Paula screeched loud in pain as Gormez kept his composure and held her tight in his arms.

"Everything is going to be alright, Sunshine. I promise you." He said rubbing the back of her head to console with genial strokes and a soft tone. He felt it was best to give her the details of he murder which caused her to break down even more. Gormez held her close to him as he helped her walk back to the ranch.

"Sara, come quickly." He yelled out to the maid from inside the house.

"Yes, Mr. Gormez. what's going on?"

"Please bring us some cold drinks.. He ordered as he helped Paula to the sofa.

Sara returned with two glasses of cold lemonade plus some Vodka for Gormez. "Is she going to be alright?"

"She'll be fine." Taking a big gulp of Voka.

Sara's concern for Paula came with much love and respect for the family. She had been with the family for over twenty- five years and helped raise Paula and Pedro after the death of their parents. She treated the two like her very own kids. During these years Sara has seen her share of drama and murder and still loved and respected the family. She did her job well and was paid well. Paula's mother and her were best friends growing up even though they were not allowed to spend much time together back then. Their relationship grew stronger over the years as they got older and were able to make their own decisions.

"Papi."

"Yes Sunshine."

"Please have the driver take me home.

"Sunshine you can stay here." Not wanting her to leave.

"I'll be fine Papi. I just need some time to myself to clear my thoughts.

"You sure, sweetheart?" Sara asked while sitting across from Gormez.

"I'm sure. I'll call or come back later this week. I just need some sleep and to clear my head." She convinced them.

"Okay Sunshine I want you to take it easy and call me when you get home.If you need anything and I mean anything let me know. I'll have it there in seconds, Sunshine."

He let her go home even though he wanted to hold her hostage like he always tried to.

"Okay Papi, I'll call you when I get home.

Gormez rose to his feet, placing the Vodka bottle down on the table and  motioned his hands to his bodyguards to escort Paula to the limo.

# CHAPTER 7

Karen was awakened by the sound of someone slurping on Italian Icey.

"Uhm damn Lisa, right there, oooh I'm cumming, uh ahhhh!" Dantwan grunted releasing cum globs into Lisa's mouth. Breathing hard as if he had just ran the fifty yard dash at full speed.

Lisa removed her mouth from Dantwan's deflating penis and spit the semen into a glass. "Did you like that?" She asked, smiling ear to ear at Dantwan.

"Ooh girl you nasty." Karen blurted out laughing.

"Take your peeping Tom ass back to sleep." Lisa said as she wiped cum off her mouth.

"Shit I want some head too." A.J. Stated as he woke up stretching and yawning looking at Karen.

"You better go get some from one of them crackhead bitches up the street then."

"Bitch you know you need to stop fronting because you know you give more head than a little bit." Lisa blurted out laughing.

"Yea my man's dick when I had one."

"I want to be your man. I want to be your man." A.J. Sang out like Roger Chapmen and the Zapp Band song.

"Hell anybody would be yo man if you could blow like Lisa." Dantwan laughed while rolling another blunt.

"Shut up boy." Lisa looked seductively at Dantwan, as his cell phone began ringing. The caller I.D. Indicated Tyson was calling. Dantwan walked into the kitchen to take the call.

"Yeah what's up."

"What you doing?" Tyson asked.

"We're just waking up." Dantwan replied as he looked into the living at Lisa. *She's not so bad after all.* He reached in the kitchen cabinet for a clean glass.

"Where are you right now."

I'm at Lisa's apartment." Dantwan regrettably replied. He knew the clowning would come.

"She finally wore your ass down."

"It ain't like that man."

"Yea yea, listen we need to meet in an hour."

"Where?"

"Ms. Hills house. Chris has been killed."

"What! Who's head we putting on the chopping board?" Dantwan played his part well.

"Meet me in an hour, alright."

Dantwan disconnected the call and let Lisa know he had to make a run. Lisa kissed him on the cheek and whispered in his ear. "Be careful." She wrapped her arms around him. "I will always love you."

A.J. walked over to Karen and tried to kiss her but Karen wasn't having it. She blocked his efforts. "Are you crazy nigga?"

"Well let me get a hug then." He said with a puppy dog look.

"A hug can't hurt." She extended her arms to him. He squeezed her tightly and backed her up to the living room wall and pressed his body against hers, grabbing her ass with both hands rolling and pumping his hips in a circular motion against her hips.

"Get the fuck off me nigga." She swung punches with her tiny fist as hard as she could. "Disgusting mothafucka." She screamed and chased him out of the room as Dantwan thought the incident was funny.

"I got some pussy y'all." He laughed.


Karen and Lisa walked back into the house as Dantwan and A.J left.

Karen flopped down on the couch sucking her teeth. Lisa sat down beside her.

"What's wrong cuz."

"Ain't nothing."

"Come on you can talk to me lil cuz."

"Its' so much I don't know where to begin."

"You like A.J. don't you?"

No. Karen lied.

"Come on girl. I know you."

"I mean he's alright. But every time I get with somebody they turn out to be running game and break my heart. The shit get old."

"Girl don't I know it. Ms. A nigga can't do shit for me. You gone break down and fall in love. Mark my words."

Lisa looked into Karen's eyes as they began to water. She reached over to grab her cousin to embrace her with a tight hug.

"Give him a try or at least give love a try. It comes in unknown places at unknown times. A guarded heart will leave you old and lonely."

They hugged each other with tears running down their faces.

- - - - -

Julio and Jesus walked through the Haywood mall in Greenville SC to meet with their inside man. As they walked into Footlocker they spotted him trying on shoes. Julio noticed that the white man with brownish rusty hair and a thin mustache with a dark blue sport jacket and slacks had a 357 magnum holstered in his jacket as he sat down beside him.

"Mego, What's the word."

"I haven't been able to get any information on Chris Hill yet. The lead detective hasn't left his office." Sergeant Santana informed. "I'm headed back to the station I'll corner him for some information then."

"Call me immediately." Julio stated as he signaled to Jesus that it was time to go.

"Remember that Mr. Gormez is very impatient man so we need that information asap."

"I'll call as soon as I get the information."

Santana sat in footlocker for five minutes to give Julio and Jesus a head start. Santana had been working for the Gormez family for the last five years providing valuable information that has kept the Gormez family business thriving. He gave Jesus the name and addresses of informants, safe houses and trial dates along with other information. All of which kept him indebted to Jesus. Santana didn't have a wife and kids that anybody knew about and spent most of his time in strip clubs and tricking money on hood tricks which after a little digging Jesus was able to use his bad habits as a threat to lure him to being his informant. But Santana always kept records of all the jobs he did for Jesus.

Joey stopped by Jackie's apartment the following day to get his belongings. Jackie's apartment was full of young thugs drinking old English 800 and smoking weed while three children sat on the worn out couch in the living room with springs sticking out of it. The little girl was playing with dead roaches while the two little boys were jumping up and down on the dangerous couch.

Joey knocked on the door.

"Who is it?" A male voice yelled throughout the house from the kitchen but Joey ignored him and knocked again, forcing the man to come to the door.

"What you want, nigga?" Larry love eyed Joey up and down with a mean look.

"It ain't like that, nigga. I just came to get my shit and dip."

"Yo Jackie!" Larry yelled for Jackie, who was upstairs going through his drug package.

"What?"

"That nigga down here."

Jackie came down the stairs cussing loud, dressed like a hooker. She had on some short shorts that revealed her ass cheeks with a fishnet top that showed her nipples. Her lips covered in red lipstick with matching sneakers.

"What you want? Didn't I tell you not to come back over here."

"That's cool. I just came to get my stuff."

"Boy I threw that shit in the dumpster. When you left your clothes left too. Now would you please leave because my man is here."

Larry walked up behind Jackie grabbing her by the waist, pressing his manhood on her ass as she grunted.

Joey looked at Larry and noticed that he had on one of his shirts. *This bitch ain't shit!* Joey stood with his feelings hurt but was damn glad that this chapter of his life was over. He felt bad for the kids having a mother like that but there was nothing he could do. He glanced at the kids once last time before leaving.

"Dont do that, get that out of your mouth."

The little girl, Lorey was putting a roach in her mouth. She immediately put it down and tried to run over to Joey for a hug. She always minded Joey, he was the only one who defended her against Jackie's punches and fed the kids whenever they were hungry. Jackie and Larry blocked her from getting to Joey.

"Joey I'm hungry." Lorey spoke in a soft sweet voice.

"Get your ass back over there on that sofa." Jackie yelled slapping her on the arm causing her to cry.

"Jackie I'll be right back." Joey stated as he walked away.

Joey went to the nearest burger joint and ordered food for the kids. Before he headed back to Jackie's he stopped at the Citgo to get drinks and hoped to see Paula but she wasn't working.

He went back to Jackie's apartment. The kids spotted him

getting out of a cab and ran to him. He gave them the bags of food and drinks he bought for their starving little bellies. While he passed out food to the older children, Lorey held on to his legs eating a fry. Jackie came out of the house and noticed the kids enjoying food that Joey bought.

"Oh no! Give him that food back." I don't need you to feed my babies. She yelled, walking towards one of her sons, knocking the hamburger to the ground.

Jacki then walked over to Joey and snatched Lorey off his leg, slapping the fry out of her hand and dragged her back to the front porch. The entire time Larry and his crew was laughing. However, no one spotted Reader in the cut watching with tears running down her face.

"Jackie its cool, I'm getting ready to roll. All I came for is my clothes but you got your boyfriend wearing my shit."

As Joey turned to walk away, Reader walked up and chimed in. "What's happening Joey." With watery eyes.

"Everything's alright. Take this and I'll holla at you later." He handed her 200 dollars.

"Damn Red you done came up."

"And I'm not falling off so you better roll with me." He said as he looked back at Jackie watching his roll of hundreds.

"Aight."

Joey. Joey. Joey. Jackie called out to him. Joey walked off smiling as he ignored Jackie cause he knew what she wanted and now she'll know she fucked up soon enough.

Reader walked off a few steps behind Joey.

"Go get yourself together babygirl. Its time to shine. I'll holla at you later. He peeled off into the woods that led to Elder street in Nichole town to meet his team.

# CHAPTER 8

Joey met up with Dantwan and Tyson at Chris mothers house with flowers and presents trying to console her. Each one of them also brought thirty-thousand dollars a piece to five Ms. Hill. Tyson also poured out two bottles of Crown Royal for their falling soldier.

As soon as Ms. Hill stepped out of the living room to use the bathroom, Tyson barked orders to meet at the stash house.

"Be careful and keep your ears and eyes open at all times because shit was getting thick."

Tyson's intentions when setting fire to the house was to dispose of any identity of Chris and Pedro's body. However, the fire wasn't enough and now they were stuck finding a way to keep the cops and the Gormez family from finding out about their involvement.

"Fella's I'm tired. I've been up all morning and need to get my rest."

Ms. Hill gave them all hugs and kissed on the cheeks. They persuaded her to take the money to take care of bills and food even though she was reluctant too she accepted their help. The men went their separate ways.

- - - - -

Paula returned to her town house. She flopped down on her couch and began thinking about Pedro as tears fell from her eyes. She grabbed her photo album off the coffee table to flip through pictures of her and Pedro. She recalled memories of him and her and how protective he was of her. She thought back to an incident in 10th grade when a boy kissed her behind the gym. Pedro beat the boy badly and broke his arms and legs. Paula screamed out for him to stop but Pedro was too enraged with anger that her screams went unheard.

Paula snapped out of her daydream and made phone call to her uncle to let him know that she was doing fine and home safely. After her talk with her uncle she grabbed a towel and wash cloth from the linen closet. Then her phone rung.

"Hello."

"May I speak with Paula please." Joey asked.

"Who's calling?"

"Joey."

"How did you get my number?"

"I pulled a few strings. It cost me a pretty penny." Joey said trying to sound sexy.

"Well I don't appreciate someone giving you my private number. If I wanted you to have it,  I would have given it to you myself." Paula snapped at Joey.

"Oh my bad, babygirl. You want have to worry about me calling again."

"I mean, I'm sorry, I had a bad day."

"Well let your boy come scoop you up and take you out somewhere nice to eat."

Paula rejected the invitation for a rain check.

"I need to shower and get some rest. I'm pretty tired. I had death in the family and I'm just not feeling myself, rain check?"

"Rain check, babygirl."

Paula grabbed her wash cloth and towel and headed for the shower. She let the shower run until the temperature was warm to touch before getting in. She stepped in the tub and let the water run down her head to her feet while she thought about Joey going through the lengths he went through to get her number. She applied soap to her wash cloth and began bathing. As she took the cloth over her whole body and between her legs, the cloth gently brushed a crossed her clit. She dropped the rag in the tub and lifted her leg, propping it on the edge of the tub. She slid her fingers up and down on her clit in slow motion before sticking two fingers inside herself. She begin to thrust her hips in a circular motion in rhythm with her fingers. She began moaning and licking her lips pumping harder against her fingers. As she began reaching her climax her legs got weak so she slowly got on her knees and aggressively rubbed her clit to reach her climax.

———-

Tony and Mike pulled up in front of Jackie's apartment and blowed the horn twice. Twenty-seconds later Larry came running out the apartment and jumped into the back seat of their truck.

"What's good man."

"You got that?" Tony asked.

"Yeah I got that but I'm a little short. Larry replied.

"Like always right."   Mike jumped into the back seat with Larry.

"What's up Tony?" Larry started to feel uneasy. But Tony didn't respond. Instead he pulled off heading out of the apartment complex.

"Don't try nothing stupid, nigga." Mike informed Larry now holding a 38 Saturday night special on Larry.

"What's going on Tony, we better than this. We go way back man." Larry had fear in his eyes.

Tony continued to drive the truck without saying one word but glancing in the rear view mirror at Larry. All Tony could think about was all the moneyLarry owe him from coming up short all these years. He counted all the drugs he fronted Larry and the money he owes him. Tony pulled over on a back street road in Nichol town and turned the truck off.

"Larry when are you going to have my 1600 dollars.

"What are you talking about man?" Apparently he didn't keep up with the count the way Tony did because he had no intentions of paying it back.

"Get the fuck out of my shit, nigga."

"What's going on man?"

"Get the fuck out of my shit nigga."

Come on man, it ain't got to be like this."

Mike slapped the 38 across Larry's face. He grabbed his face and screamed.

"I can't see. As he fell against the truck door.

Tony and Mike began laughing. Tony snatched the baseball bat from the trunk while Larry was trying to recuperate from the blow of the 38. As soon as Larry regained his vision and posture Tony swung the bat hitting Larry in the neck causing him to grab his throat gasping for air. Causing the 190 pounds of muscle to drop to his knees. Larry still had enough strength to get up on his feet. He tried to flee but caught a right hook from Mike then both Mike and Larry laid punches on him until they were tired.

"Get my mothafucking money." Tony stumped Larry in the face knocking his grill lose. Mike fired off a bullet into Larry's leg. They left Larry in a pool of his own blood, with a broken arm and shoulder, busted ear drum, swollen eyes and nose. Tony yelled out of the truck before pulling off.

"Have my money by tomorrow, nigga or the next time I'm going to kill you."

- - - - -

Detective I hear that they are down stairs booking the Timothy Park Rapist serial killer."

Santana stated leaning on Detectives Hoffman's office door.

"What, where they catch him at? That was my case. I'll be right back."

Hoffman replied standing up from his desk and rushing out of his office leaving Santana standing by the door.

Santana knew that he only has a few minutes to get the information concerning Chris Hill before Hoffman returned raising hell and cussing him out for lying about the Timothy Park rapist. Santana went to Hoffman's desk and opened his files and hit the jack pot when he saw in bold Chris Hill/Pedro Gormez written on a folder.

Santana grabbed his phone and began taking pictures of the files containing addresses and other important information. He finished taking snapshots just in time to see Hoffman rushing back into the office.

"What are you doing at my desk, Santana?"

"Nothing I was just walking past. I see they put you on that double homicide case."

Hoffman didn't acknowledge Santana question. But he did make a mental note to run a background on Santana. He always felt a bad vibe about him and now he's snooping at his desk.

"Well, Hoffman I have to go. Seems like the boss wants me and a couple of other officers to babysit informants.

"Alright, good luck. He dropped his head down into his paperwork.

# CHAPTER 9

Tyson, Joey, and Dantwan met at the one bedroom house where they stashed the bricks of cocaine the night before. Dantwan and Tyson sat down at the small table in the kitchen while Joey went to retrieve the stash from the stash loaded in trash bags from the back bedroom. Joey came back into the kitchen and began pulling Kilos of cocaine sealed in plastic wrap onto the table. The smell of cocaine hit their noses like grandma's cooking. They counted 17 bricks in all.

"Yea nigga, we got off." Dantwan beamed in happiness as he lined the bricks in a row.

As they began to split the bricks open Joey noticed a difference between them. "Yo Ty them two bricks there look different."

"Let me see" Tyson grabbed one of the bricks. He broke the seal with his pinky nail and scooped a line of grain and placed it on his tongue. "Oh Shit!"

"What's wrong?" Joey jumped.

"Boys I believe we hit the jack pot!" Tyson could see dollar signs.

"What are you talking about man?" Dantwan asked.

"What we have here partner is one hungdred percent uncut raw heroin." Wishing he had some cigars to pass around.

Although, Joey and Dantwan was not familiar with selling heroin they knew it brought a lot of money of which was now at their finger tips.

"Listen up fellas. We have knocked off some major players. I don't know who they are but you can be sure they are coming to for their shit. We got to be real careful not to draw attention to ourselves. No splurging! Each one of us gets a brick to hustle on the low until this shit blows over. And as far as the raw dog food, we are not touching it right now. Let's put this up for a rainy day, do y'all understand?" Tyson continued to lay down the plan. Now let's break one of these keys down. Dantwan is going to take half to put up. Joey you take the other half and stash it. I'll take this whole key to put it under lock and key. By no means, what so ever, are we to tamper with this dog food until I say its time to move it. Pass me the gloves and a mask and let's get to work."

- - - - -

Julio and Papi received a phone call from Sergeant Santana to meet him at Zobra Loung Restaurant off Laurens Road and East Washington Street. When they arrived they waited in their car for five minutes before they entered the restaurant. Santana was sitting in the back corner drinking a Scotch on the rocks.

"Hey guys, y'all want a drink." Santana offered as Julio and Papi approached his table. The men sat down with open ears not interested in drinking with Santana.

"I got some information that might be interesting." Santana said half tipsy rocking to the rhythm of a country song playing on the Jukebox.

"Spill it." Papi sighed not wanting to be around Santana longer than he had to.

Santana pulled some paper work from his jacket pocket and laid them across the table. Julio picked up some of the paper work and began reviewing the paper work. "What's this Santana?"

"Well, this is the information I received from the head investigator of the case and right there on this sheet is a list of names that Chris Hill was associated with or at least knew him or he knew them. There on this side is Chris Hill's mother's address. We don't know if he lived with her but that's the only address we have on him right now."

Who is this Joey Knight guy right here." Julio pointed his finger at the name listed as close friends and family of Chris Hill.

"We have not questioned anybody yet but you have to understand that this is not my case so I have to be real careful but as soon as I find out more information, I will keep y'all posted." Santana sipped on his drink.

"You do that but in the mean time we will check into who is who." Julio replied as him and Papi stood up and began walking off from the table leaving Santana sitting there looking at their backs.

After Santana finished his drink she dropped a tip on the table along with the tab fee. He almost lost his balance but caught himself and began staggering towards the front door. He stood in front of his car and pulled a twenty out of his wallet before putting it into his trunk. He tucked the twenty into his front pocket and peeled off towards Laurens road.

- - - - -

"Bitch when I catch you I'm going to fuck you up!" Jackie screamed after Reader who was running down the street.

"Fuck you!" Reader shouted back with one foot in front of the other. Knowing that if Jackie caught her 100 pounds of flesh and bones it was over with. She would over power her, easily.

After Reader turned the corner of the building, Jackie gave up and stormed back into her apartment slamming the screen door behind her cussing and scaring the children. She went upstairs and slammed her bedroom door mad as hell because Reader would not give her half the money Joey gave her.

As Jackie laid back on her bed she slid down with head resting on her pillow thinking about the knot of cash Joey had.

*Where did he get all of that money. Damn I fucked up! I gave him my ass to kiss and his clothes away for a nigga I don't give a damn about, a great fuck and a lil change. Somebody I can get high with. Shit I got to get my boo back fast.*

She thought about using the kids to get him to come around because she knew he loved them and would do anything for them. Or maybe manipulate Larry with some good ass and head and a little pillow talk, to get him to rob Joey and they split the money.

She heard a loud bang down stairs and the children crying so she got up from her bed and ran downstairs. The children were crying and pointing at Larry, stretched out on the couch bleeding. Jackie immediately ran out the front door calling for Larry homeboys to come help her with Larry.

- - - - -

Reader made it to the crack house in the middle court in Fieldcrest away from Jackie's wrath. She was in her comfort zone putting holders on a twelve ounce Pepsi Cola bottle with aluminum foil tapped around the top of the bottle with a small hole punched in the aluminum foil and the crack placed in the middle sitting on cigarette ashes. As Reader struck the burned out lighter and placed it to the bottle placing the flame of the lighter on the white hard substance and inhaled through a hole in the side of the bottle. Reader inhaled the crack smoke knowing her last 40 dollars were well spent.

The other fiends gathered around her asking for the smoke in the bottles while others had their finger tips glued to every white spot on the floor. One of the fiends stood peeping out the side window announced that someone was coming. The jittery fiends jumped at the sound of the knock on the door. The fiend who lurked near the window had a knife in his hand scared, thinking someone was after him.

The Mexicans walked into the crack house with their noses in the air. "Hey Mego, I got this hundred dollar bill here for anybody who can tell me where Joey Knight is at." Julio tempted the fiends. The fiends looked around at each other but didn't know anyone by Joey Knight, as they only knew him by Big Red. Reader was the only one there who knew his real name because they went to school together. Reader was tempted knowing she just spent her last 40 dollars. The rest of the fiends gathered around plotting how to take the hundred dollars from Julio.

Julio noticed the look in their eyes and that no one was giving up Joey. He pulled out his gun and the fiends retreated to their search for crumbs of crack on the floor.

- - - - -

Paula was awakened by her alarm clock. She reached over to the side of her bed and hit the button stopping the loud irritating noise. As she raised out of her bed still laying in the nude, she glanced over at the clock, Oh shit I'm going to be late. Paula jumped up and ran to the bathroom to brush her teeth and put on her work uniform. A pair of black slacks and black, red, and white company shirt. After gathering everything she needed she grabbed her keys to her Jeep and walked out of the house. She arrived at work fifteen minutes later and began restocking the shelves preparing for the eleven o'clock rush hour when the plants nearby switched shifts. The employees coming and going caused a major rush hour. Standing behind the cash register she noticed two young black females exiting a chrome out infinity sitting on twenty- six inch rims. The two guys pushing the ship were Tony and Mike. They went straight to the beer cooler before proceeding to the counter.

"Can you put two packs of Newport's and a box of swisher sweet perfectos with that. Tony stated.

"Yes Sir, that will be $29.42."

Tony handed Paula two twenty dollar bills.

"Thank you very much for your service, Please come back." She handed Tony his change.

As they drove out of the parking lot, stopping for a stop sign , Joey, and Dantwan was pulling into the Citgo. Tyson parked next to a pay phone.

"I'll be right back, y'all want anything?" Joey asked while getting out of the car.

"Yeah, bring a six pack of something. Dantwan said, staring at the car sitting at the stop sign.

"I'm cool." Tyson got out of the car to use the pay phone.

Joey walked into the store as Tyson got back into the car after his phone call went to voicemail.

"You see that car?" Dantwan asked Tyson, trying to figure out where he knew it from.

"Hell everybody in town got a car like that."

Joey came back holding a six pack of Coors Light under his right arm smiling ear to ear.

"Damn nigga, what you so cheesy for?" Dantwan asked while Tyson checked the surrounding for cops, stick up boys, informants...etc because they were riding dirty. He still had 2 Kilos strapped to him along with 3 bricks and their automatics in the car. Not waiting around he started the car.

"I'm about to lock that honey in the store." Joey was still smiling thinking about Paula's smile.

"What happened to crazy ass Jackie, that Fieldcrest chic?" Tyson knowing he just dropped Joey off there the night before.

"That bitch history." He began explaining how things went down between him and her.

"Man I would have kicked that bitch face off. She wouldn't have tried me like that." Dantwan always thought he was above any and everything.

"Nah man, It's cool. I crushed that bitch when she seen my knot of hundreds when I gave her cousin some money. The bitch had the nerve to call out for me."

Tyson couldn't believe his ears. "You did what?

"Who is her peeps? Dantwan chimed in.

"Y'all know, Reader." Cracking another beer open.

"Y'all niggas must think it's a game. We riding around dirty as hell and y'all opening beers, having a party like it's nothing. Like we can jump out and run if we get pulled over with all this heat and dope on us."

"Chill out man we in the hood now." Dantwan popped an

attitude.

"Anyway. Joey you mean the same Reader that you and Chris got to fighting over in elementary school, that dissed both of y'all then y'all ganged her." Tyson changed the subject back to Reader to avoid snapping on Dantwan.

"Yeh, that Reader." He smirked, "Make a right turn at the corner of Maco Street in Nichol town.

"Ty drop me off down at Lisa's apartment after you drop Joey off. I believe I am getting ready to put her on the team."

"I think that's a good idea. You might want to stash that half of brick at her crib. You think she can handle it.

"Yeh Ty. I got that on lock. If I told her to jump she would say how high daddy. He bragged and gave a big smile showing his gold teeth and they all joined in laughter.

# CHAPTER 10

The following week the family had Chris Hill's funeral and across town Mr. Gormez had Pedro's funeral. Funny thing four women showed up at Chris's funeral wearing black dresses, each holding a baby in their arms, claiming the kid was Chris's. Poor Ms. Hill fainted and it took several people to help her up and calm her down.

Tyson and Tonya sat in the second row while Joey sat next to meMs. Hill holding her hand, with her head resting on his shoulder, crying that she'll never see her son again.

Dantwan and A.J. accompanied by Lisa and Karen stood against the back wall near the entrance. Tyson made it clear to watch the surrounding for any unfamiliar faces and police officers. Detective Hoffman parked across the street taking pictures of everybody who entered, trying to put his case together. Dantwan noticed two Mexican men standing in the corner watching Joey and Ms. Hill. He whispered to A.J. to deliver a message to Tyson to meet him in the bathroom immediately. A.J. told Karen to deliver the message. Karen sat behind Tonya and delivered the message for her to deliver to Tyson.

Just before Dantwan moved from his spot he saw Jackie sitting in the fifth row with a short as dress on, putting on a front with tears in her eyes. She hated Chris. They couldn't stand each another. They always argued and at one point he thought they were fucking behind his back. But then realized that his right hand man didn't get down like that.

When Karen returned Dantwan made his way to the bathroom to wait on Tyson.

"What's up?" Tyson went into an empty stale.

"I seen two Mexicans in there looking and taking pictures of Ms. Hill and Joey. Dantwan began running water in the sink so that nobody could hear their conversation outside the door.

"Yea I saw them too. Don't worry I got a plan."

"What are you going to do?"

"Some things are better left unsaid. Just let me handle it."

"Alright." Dantwan heard the anger in Tyson's voice and decided to leave it at that. "Let's get back out there before they start missing us." He turned the water off.

"You go ahead. I got to take a shit then make a quick run across town. I'll meet y'all at the burial site." Tyson place toilet paper around the toilet seat and sat down.

"Alright I'll see you at the burial sight then."

- - - - -

Mr. Gormez and his crew of bodyguards got out of a pearl white limousine, that was followed by several black limousines. Accompanying Mr. Gormez on his left arm was Sara, while Paula held tight to his right arm. Three of his bodyguards stood watch while the family stood around Pedro's closed casket before being lowered into the ground. The preacher said a couple of words followed by an emotional outburst by a young Mexican girl named Anna. After falling to the ground yelling and historically crying with her son lil Pedro hugging her leg while sucking his thumb, Mr. Gormez had her removed from the premises.

Soon after Anna was escorted to her car, dark clouds formed as thunder, lightening and rain filled the sky. Family and friends stood a few minutes more under umbrellas paying their respects before leaving. Mr. Gormez stood thinking if the life that he lived was worth all the body counts in his family. He had already lost his brother and sister and now his nephew to this lifestyle. His thoughts were interrupted by his bodyguard who guided him off to the side from crowd.

"Sir you have a call."

"Speak to me."

"The information that we received from Santana has checked out. We just left the funeral home of the deceased party that was found with Pedro's body. Me and Papi are going to tail the guy to see what we come across."

"Julio, keep me posted."

- - - - -

Larry came back from the hospital banged and bandaged up. Larry was still trying to figure out how his tab got up to sixteen hundred dollars. He also had no idea how he was going to come up with the money to pay Tony. Jackie walked into the apartment and looked at Larry. What a worthless piece of shit.

But she had to use him to get to make a move a Joey. At the funeral she had approached Joey telling him that the children been asking about him and saying they miss him, her included. Joey already peeped her game so he immediately dissed her in front of everybody. Joey made a spectacle out of Jackie with a few jokes that his homeboys and ladies laughed at. Of course Jackie didn't expect that from the man who once loved her and would do anything for her. Jackie being Jackie didn't let on that Joeys rejection and jokes got to her. She retreated but knew what she had to do.

Jackie began rubbing on Larry's manhood before unzipping his zipper to release his beef from his pants. She slowly stroked it as beef expanded in her hand. She spit on the tip and slowly wrapped her lips around it, slid her lips on top guiding his tip to the back of her throat. His dick giggled her throat as her mouth filled with saliva. She let her tong make love to Larry's dick and he enjoyed every minute of it.

"Oooh yeahhhh." Larry grunted while he pumped his hips back and forth.

Jackie picked up the past causing Larry to reach climax quickly.

"Uhhh as he released his sperm into Jackie's mouth. Jackie caught all of Larry's sperm, titled her head back and gargled then swallowed. Larry looked on with lust in his eyes, he loved that shit. " Girl, I love you."

*Jack pot!*

- - - - -

Lisa and Karen decided not to sit through the entire funeral.

They returned back to Lisa's apartment in Roosevelt.

"Karen, you see how Joey dogged that bitch?"

"That couldn't have been me. I would've showed my ass on that nigga."

"Girl you don't even know the other half. That bitch Jackie crazier than a motherfucker. She stay into some shit starting drama."

"He still didn't have to do her like that." Karen grabbed a bottle of grey goose and began to take a sip. Suddenly, a knock at the door, "Who is it?"

"Come see." A male voice teased.

Lisa stumped to the front door saying a few profane words as she snatched the door open and there stood Tony and Mike, smiling ear to ear.

"How y'all ladies doing today." Tony entered the apartment without being invited in.

Dantwan had already told Lisa not to have no one in her apartment because he had the heroin and some coke stashed there and if he and A.J. showed up, all hell would break loose.

"So what y'all up too." Karen asked looking at Mike thinking about the date he promised to take her on.

"We just trying to find some place to chill and blaze a couple of blunts. Tony pulled out an ounce of weed and two blunts.

"Well y'all can't do it here." Karen, Tony, and Mike looked at Lisa like she was crazy. Not believing that she was really trying to kick them out.

"What's up Lisa you flipping on yo boy." Tony smirked.

"No I'm just getting ready to take a nap because I have to go handle some business in an hour."

"Oh I see what's going on." Tony picking for information.

"Ain't nothing going on. Now is not a good time."

"Yea aight." Tony felt like since she kicked them out for Dantwan and A.J. she got distant with him. Not answering his calls and brushing him off when he came by. "Let me use the bathroom first?"

Tony went to the bathroom and checked his appearance in the mirror and saw a few bumps on his face. He looked in the medicine cabinet to see if Lisa had some kind of ointment or some medicated wipes. He didn't see anything that could help in the medicine cabinet so he checked the bottom cabinet. *What's this?* He saw a block of white substance wrapped in plastic wrap so he unwrapped it. Jack pot! He found Dantwan stash and tucked it in his pants around his waist line. He flushed the toilet and scurried out of the bathroom.

"Aight Mike lets be out. Ladies don't go into the bathroom anytime soon, it's hazardous in there."

"You nasty boy. Go on somewhere." Karen laughed.

Before leaving out the door Tony looked Lisa in the eyes, "I'll holla at you later." With a sneaky smile.

# CHAPTER 11

Tyson was sitting on the toilet taking a shit when he heard two men enter the restroom. Tyson listened in closely to the sound of their accents and he could tell they were Mexicans. He raised his feet to avoid them knowing that he was in there. He listened closely.

"Make the phone call." One of them spoke.

The man called the person on the other end Sir and mentioned Ms. Hill and Joey's name. "Me and Papi are going to tail the guy to see what we come across." The news must have satisfied the recipient on the other end because the men immediately left out of the bathroom.

Tyson knew he needed to act quick. He went back into the open service and whispered to Dantwan to tell Joey to drive to Timothy Park off Highway 25 immediately after the service. Joey arrived at Timothy Park, the same place Tyson had murdered and buried Ray Ray. He walked over to a bench to sit down just as he spotted Tyson standing in the wooded pathway a few feet ahead. Tyson disappeared as quickly as he appeared and Joey knew to follow. Joey searched for Tyson not knowing he was sitting in the top of a tree watching Joey being trailed by Julio and Papi.

"Where this fucker going? Show us the money mothafucker."

Julio entered the path behind Joey while Papi was walking a few steps behind him. Joey slowed his pace in search for Tyson.

The men caught up to Joey with their guns drawn. "Stop right there and don't try no funny business or you a dead man."

"Here you can have everything, just don't shoot man."

Julio and Papi laughed because they had no intentions on robbing Joey.

"Our boss Mr. Gormez would like a word with you. Let's go." He motioned for Joey to turn and walk in the direction of the cars. At that moment Tyson revealed himself holding two 45's with silencers.

"Don't move wetbacks or I'll blow your shit off."

Julio and Papi turned around to face Tyson. Papi reached for his gun at the same time Joey let one rip and put one in Papi's head. He hit the ground with a thump.

"Grab your friends legs and drag him over here." Tyson ordered Julio deeper into the woods near Ray Ray's dead body. "Put your friend over there next to that body."

Julio and Joey's eyes got big when they saw Ray Ray's body laying there and the smell turned their stomachs. Julio then knew he was a dead man. Once he let go of Papi's legs, Tyson put two rounds to the back of his head.

"Help me put these leaves and twigs over these mothafuckas." They began concealing the bodies before them. Once they finished Tyson told Joey he'll catch up with him later and took off running through the woods. Leaving Joey pondering what the hell just happened.

- - - - -

"Yeah nigga, I knew them bitches was holding for them niggas." Tony pulled out the stash to show Mike.

"Boy that look like a key and half."

"We about to get this money." Tony smiled, ear to ear as Mike examined the powder noticing two different colors.

"Damn this look like two different powders. Oh this must be the butter baby." Mike let the window down to let some fresh air in.

"You think we can go back to your crib to cook and bag this shit up." Making a left turn on Arden Street in Nichol Town.

"If that stupid ass bitch Trina ain't there, we good. You know we got to fighting this morning when I came in."

"We can go over to that crackhead apartment in fieldcrest. What's her name...uhm?"

"Who Reader?"

"Yeah Reader. Plus I heard she can cook her ass off. Make a baby eight look like a half a brick." Tony laughed.

"Shid you think she at home?"

Tony reached Rebecca Street stopping at the four way and made a left towards Fieldcrest. "We bout to find out." Tony pulled into the apartment complex and parked in the court across from Readers apartment. They walked across the street to Readers back door. As they knocked on her door they noticed someone peeking out of the curtains.

"Open the door with yo crazy ass." Mike shouted.

Mike and Tony welcomed themselves in as Reader opened the door.

"Anybody in here?" Tony looked around.

"No, why?" Reader snapped because she didn't like Tony and Mike too much and had good reasons too.

"Well, don't let nobody in here. We about to cook this shit and bag it up." Tony instructed as Mike pulled the dope out of his jacket.

Readers mouth dropped to the floor at the sight of all the cocaine. Her mouth began to water at the thought of getting high. She agreed because she knew they would break her off with something for letting them us her kitchen. Tony dumped some of the powder on the kitchen table, tasted it and then dumped a little from the other bag that looked brown then tasted a bit of that too. He immediately stopped.

"We need to talk now!"

"What's up nigga?"

"Reader go to the store and buy some beer and plastic bags."

"Okay where the money?"

Tony gave Reader a twenty dollar bill and told her to bring his change and a receipt back. As she exited the back door Tony turned his attention to Mike.

"Man we got some pure heroin right here." Handing the brown powder to Mike.

"Damn dog. We about to blow up."

You know how to cut this shit?"

"Nah but I have a cousin who shoots and sniffs this shit. I bet he knows how to cut it."

"Well we need to get out of here and get to your cousin asap."

"What about Reader and this cocaine. You know them runners

over there waiting. You can hit them off with some work."

"Yeh yeh when she come back we will cook and bag it up. In the meantime, take my cell and track down your cousin."

- - - - -

Reader caught a ride to the Citgo station to get the beer. When she walked into the store she saw Joey at the counter talking to the store clerk.

"What's good Reader."

"Ain't nothing Red. That crazy bitch Jackie robbed me for the two hundred you gave me." She lied as she walked to the beer then to the counter.

"For real." He believed her because he's seen Jackie take her welfare check and not give her a dime of it

"Well soon as I leave here I'm coming by your apartment. I got something for you."

"Give me about two hours though. I have to run somewhere for my grandmother." She lied again because she knew she couldn't pass up on what Tony and Mike was about to give her.

Joey cell began ringing while Paula was ringing up the beer Reader placed on the counter.

"Tell it."

"Man them fagot ass niggas got my stash." Dantwan yelled from the other end of the phone.

"Who!"

"Some niggas, me and A.J. bumped heads with the other night at Lisa's apartment. Some niggas name Tony and Mike.

"Hold on for a minute Dee." He covered the receiver with his hand. "Aye Reader you know some niggas name Tony and Mike. He got Readers attention as she was exciting the store.

"Yeh I know em. Why?"

"Have you seen them lately?"

Reader hesitated to answer for a minute before realizing that the man who asked always showed her respect and treated her like a decent human being instead of a low life dope fiend like Tony and Mike. She remembered when how Tony and Mike did her dirty on several occasions. She thought about a time when she was chronic and needed a fix bad. She asked Tony and Mike for a hit to get the monkey off her back. They told her if she sucked their pit bull dick they would give her an eight ball of crack which she refused. And when she walked up the street, she saw Joey and he came through for her like he always did when he could. He even came by her apartment later that night to check on her and gave her 2 more cracks. He was always a friend to her since elementary school. Even after him and Chris ganged her.

"Them mothafuckas at my apartment right now with a bunch of cocaine."

Paula heard Reader and cut her eyes at Joey.

"Hold on a second Reader." Joey removed his hand from the receiver. "Dee I know where them nigga's at."

Joey was interrupted in mid sentence by Paula. "What's going on Joey? Don't go getting into no trouble, I wouldn't like that."

"Nah, I'm good. Just got to handle some business. We still on for tomorrow morning when you get off right?"

"Yeah boo take it easy." She smiled at Joey, as he left the store.

"Reader hop in the car with me."

Joey got back to Dantwan on the other end of the phone. "Meet me in Fieldcrest." Joey waited in the car parked across the street from Readers apartment. A.J. And Dantwan showed up 10 minutes later. They began discussing their plan to get Dantwan shit back.

Reader pointed out Tony's Infinity sitting on chrome wheels. "I hope y'all don't have my apartment on News Channel 4 tonight. Reader got worried being caught in the middle of their bullshit.

"Don't worry I go you babygirl. I got a better plan for them niggas. Joey stated looking at Tony's infinity.

## CHAPTER 12

Mr. Gormez sat at his lake house wondering why Julio and Papi haven't checked in with information. He ordered his bodyguard to call Julio's and Papi's cellphone but didn't receive an answer. He became irritated and ordered Sara to bring him a glass of white wine and several shots of Vodka. Sitting in his office gulping down hots of Vodka his phone began ringing.

"Tell me something good."

"This is Santana." Santana cleared his throat preparing to deliver the bad news.

"Yeah what is it Santana."

"Sir Papi and Julio are dead. We found three bodies at Timothy Park off Highway 25."

"What!"

"Sir the bodies were found by an old white woman and her two dogs…"

"Kill the mute!" Gomez interrupted the eager Santana, hoping that this new information would help him move up in rank.

"Sir we can't. Too many clean coats are out here at the moment but I'm hot on the trail and will keep you posted."

"Wait who is the other body?"

"We just found out his name is Raymond Hall a.k.a Ray Ray.

Do you know him?"

"Don't you ever question me!"

"I'm sorry sir. What do you want me to do?"

"Two of my lieutenants are coming to speak with you. They'll be contacting your cell soon. Also Santana make sure Julio and Papi associations with me don't leak out. Do you understand?"

Santana had his ears glued to the phone. He knew Gormez meant business and had connections all over. "Yes, Sir." Santana walked back over to the crime scene unaware that he was being watched by Detective Hoffman standing behind a tree.

- - - - -

Tyson was at home with Tonya eating a T-bone steak and baked potato, watching the Channel 4 news about the triple murder in Timothy's parts. The news reporter stated that the police didn't have any suspects in connection with the murders but suspected that the Timothy Park rapist and murderer was at it again.

"Hey baby your phone ringing."

Tyson answered, "Burger King can I help you."

"Yo, man my whopper is no good and the fries are cold. Joey talked in code.

"Can you handle it yourself?"

"Yeah, without a problem." Joey responded, feeling good that Tyson finally trusted him to take care of a problem on his own.

"Was it too much ketchup?"

"They took the onions and no lettuce."

"Aight. Handle your business and don't get caught."

Tonya put her hands on her hips. "You getting ready to go somewhere aren't you?" Getting mad because he promised to stay in tonight.

"No baby. I told you that I was in for tonight." He wrapped his arms around her waist and gave her a forehead kiss.

- - - - -

While Tyson and Joey were having their conversation, Mike was on Tony's cell phone talking to his cousin Hound. Hound was an old school heroine pusher who started using his own product. He knew how to cut and move heroine because he used to hang with some big cats back in his days. Mike handed Tony the phone so he could talk to his cousin. He let Hound know that they needed him and would be at his spot in twenty minutes.

Reader came through the back door of her apartment just as Tony hung up with Hound. She placed the beer on the table.

"What's up boys?"

"We're about to get up outta here. We're gonna hold up on cooking and bagging this dope."

"Damn every time I fuck with ya'll nigga's I get shitted on."

"It ain't like that girl. We got some important business we need to handle." Mike smoothed over.

"Well what are y'all going to do for me? Let me get something for my time, nigga."

Tony smirked as he patted his pockets like he didn't have any money.

"That's alright. I'm straight, get the fuck out my house and don't come back!

Tony and Mike began walking to the back door talking shit but Reader didn't pay them no mind. She quickly locked the door and braced herself for the gunfire she was about to hear.

"Girl those niggas ain't shit." Karen stated to Lisa, who was sitting on the couch with a busted lip and swollen right eye from Dantwan left hook.

"If it wasn't for you inviting them nigga's in, none of this shit would've have happened.

"Don't be blaming me. Those nigga's walked right in. Plus Dantwan ain't all that anyway."

"You know what Karen I'm tired of your funky ass attitude. You need to find you somewhere else to live. I don't have to take this shit from you. She stared Karen in the face.

"Oh it's like that now!"

"Just like that. So get the fuck out my shit!" Lisa stood up from the couch.

"Well, fuck you too bitch." Karen rushed to the back room to get her belongings.

- - - - -

Lisa couldn't handle Dantwan but she was damn sure that she wouldn't let a hundred and ten pounds Karen do nothing to her. While Karen packed her things she realized that she didn't have nowhere to go. Knowing that she was still on the run from the police for failure to appear in court on shop lifting charges and a marijuana charge. With no money and no place to stay, Karen knew her best bet was to apologize to her cousin.

"Lisa I'm sorry." With tears in her eyes she let Lisa know that she had no where to go. Karen began telling Lisa about the last three years of her life. She told Lisa the real reason why she had to come live with her. The old 65 years old man she lived with died. For three years she fucked him and plotted on his riches only for him to leave everything to his daughter and grandson. His daughter kicked her out with nothing but a bus ticket to Greenville.

"Lisa I was never in New York. I lived with this man right here in South Carolina in Newberry. Girl I felt like a total fool. I'm sorry I lied about everything." Karen cried on Lisa's shoulders and Lisa knew she couldn't kick her little cousin out.

"Gil put your things back in your room."

"Lisa there's something else I have to tell you. But promise you wont get mad."

# CHAPTER 13

Jackie and Larry laid in the bed pillow talking about the sex they just had. All of a sudden Jackie blurted out, I hate that motherfucker and he might be the answer to yo problem!"

"Who?"

"That bitch nigga Joey."

"I thought its over with y'all. You still got feelings for that nigga?"

"Don't start with me."

"You know the other day that nigga had a knot of hundred dollar bills man."

"Ok AND!"

"And you owe Mike and Tony. They gone bust yo ass if you don't pay them. Joey baby that's your lit."

"Girl is you crazy?" Larry dismissed Jackie but began thinking Jackie might be on to something.

Jackie interrupted Larry's thoughts with a stroke on his manhood but Larry pushed her hand away.

"Damn girl chill for a minute. Ain't you tired?"

Jackie snatched her hand away from Larry and put it back in position squeezing his manhood hard, while looking him in the eyes with a smirk on her face. Larry laid stiff scared to move. Then

Jackie released her grip and began jacking Larry's rod until it became hard. When Larry was at full erection she straddled him and went for a ride. Aggressively bouncing up and down while tightening her pussy muscles, she taunted Larry until he gave in.

"You gone lick that nigga for mama?"

"Anything for you baby." He moaned.

"Promise baby?" Jackie bounced harder and faster.

"Yeah baby, I I I pppromise." Larry grunted as he began to climax. Hell yea baby."

He exploded inside of Jackie as she threw her head back in ecstasy and smiled a devious smile because she knew she had him exactly where she wanted him. After he came she laid beside him looking into his eyes as he caught his breath.

"So when are you going to do it?"

"Do what?"

"Rob Joey for me."

"How you wanna do it? You got a plan?"

Jackie smiled as she began discussing her plan with him ,to rob Joey and she wanted it done tomorrow. And soon after they both feel asleep exhausted.


Across town the phone rang exactly four times before Tonya answered it.

"Is Tyson home?" A female voice spoke.

"May I ask who the hell is this."

"I am sorry for calling your home at this time of night but it's nothing between me and your man. This is important. My husband Raymond Hall told me to call Tyson in times of an emergency. I haven't seen nor heard from my husband in three days so I need to speak to Tyson.

"Ms. Hall please hold for a minute let me wake up, Ty." Tonya walked into the bedroom where Tyson laid peacefully sleeping. She stared at him briefly before waking him. Thinking about how if he was missing she would tear the city up looking for him. She nudged Tyson to wake him up and let him know Ray's wife is on the phone.

"Hello Tyson speaking."

"Tyson this is Brenda Hall. I haven't seen nor heard from Raymond in three days. Have you seen him?" Praying that Tyson had some information to put her mind at ease.

"No, I haven't see nor heard from him either. I've been waiting on him to contact me about some business.

"Tyson, I believe something bad has happened to him. She blurted out crying.

" Mrs. Hall don't worry. Let me reach out to some people first thing in the morning. But if you hear from him before I contact you, please have him call me asap." Tyson feeling bad for having to kill Ray, leaving his wife behind emotionally dysfunctional.

"Please find my husband and bring him home in good health."

"I'll try my best. Just stay strong and get some sleep." Tyson hung up the phone.

"Baby what's going on?" Tonya asked Tyson.

"Ain't nothing going on. Rays' wife looking for him. He's probably laid up with that young tender Roni he's been creeping with."

"Um hmm. Tonya pushed Tyson's leg and arm aside so that she

could get in the bed to watch some T.V. Before falling off to sleep.

- - - - -

Sergeant Santana sat waiting in Haywood Mall's food court for Carlos and Shantez, Mr. Gormez's lieutenants. While stuffing his mouth with pizza he heard a voice behind him.

"Follow us. Keep your distance."

Santana stood up and began following the two men. Not knowing that they were being tailed by Detective Hoffman's investigator, Johnny Paden, who snapped pictures and carried a recorder hoping to record their conversation, even from thirty feet away.

Carlos and Sanchez led Santana into the shafts of Haywood Mall that led them to the back of the department stores. They stopped at an off brand store and proceeded to the back office where Mr. Gormez greeted Santana with an extended hand. It wasn't in Gormez's nature to meet with corrupted cops but this was a special occasion but he had plans of promoting Santana to a higher rank if Santana came through with useful information.

Paden lost his trail as the men entered the shaft tunnels. So he decided to go back to his car which was parked five cars down from Santana's car. While waiting he decided to contact Hoffman.

"I have been following Santana all day as you requested. He meet with two Mexican men, well dressed and muscular. Santana followed them into the mall shafts tunnel and I lost them. I'm waiting in the car once I have more information I will let you know. Before disconnecting the call he jotted something down on his notepad.


"I had to meet you face to face which is against my own policy. So I' am taking a chance with you. Do you understand Sergeant? Mr. Gormez stated in a calm fashion.

"Yes Sir." Santana said.

"What information do you have for me?"

"Sir to be honest, nobody knows what the hell is going on. Bodies keep piling up. Keep your family members close and protected by all means. "

"Do you think it's another mob family?" Gormez asked concerned.

"I can't say for sure but it's better to be safe then sorry."

"Excuse me for a second Sergeant." Gormez turned to Carlos. "Call and have someone pick up Paula."

As Gormez gave instructions another one of his men came into the office and whispered to Gormez. Gormez then turned his attention back to Santana.

"You got flees on you man."

"What are you talking about?"

"You have someone following you. Sitting in the parking lot waiting for you to return."

"Yeah I noticed the tail a few blocks back on my way here."

"Do you think he is a problem?"

"Maybe, maybe not." Santana didn't know who was tailing him.

"Well just in case, I'll send somebody to silence him now."

Mr. Grmez called for another one of his men and to go with

Carlos and Shantez to handle the detective and find out what he knows.

"Fellas make sure to send his dead body back to whoever sent him."

# CHAPTER 14

After Tony and Mike came out of Readers house they proceeded across the street to their car. Tony tossed Mike the keys to drive. As soon as Mike stuck the key into the car door they were ambushed with flying bullets from Dantwan's nine millimeter. One of the slugs hit Mike in the neck. Tony immediately pulled out a mini Uzi and began firing back. Tat tat tat tat catching A.J. below the waist line.

Joey took cover beside a nearby car and fired two shots from his Glock 40 hitting Tony's car windshield, as glass shattered everywhere. Reader peeped out her window with a smile on her face, mixed with concern hoping that Joey wouldn't get hurt. People nearby took cover while the other dope boys drew their weapons to prepare to shoot if someone came their way.

Jackie and Larry were also awaken from their sleep and went to the window to see what was going on. As they watched from her bedroom window, they saw Joey stand up from behind a car aiming and firing at his target, as Dantwan stood over Mike and dumped rounds into him.

"Take this nigga!

After Dantwan emptied his clip into Mike he went over to A.J. to help him off the ground. Joey took off after Tony. From a distance you could hear their guns exchanging fire.

Dantwan helped A.J. into the back of the car and took off in the direction of the gunfire. He spotted Joey and blew the horn. Joey noticed it was Dantwan and ran to the car and jumped in the passenger side.

Tony was breathing hard and almost out of breath as he pulled the bag of product from his pants because it had started to slip while he was running. Tony's adrenaline was still pumping fast but he knew he needed to keep moving and get to a hiding place fast. He didn't know who was after him and where the fuck they came from. He thought about his best-friend Mike and shed a tear for his fallen comrade. They went back a long ways since the age of three. Their mothers used to hang together. Mike even did a three year bid for something Tony did and never ratted him out. Tony got angrier as he thought about losing his friend. *"I swear somebody gone pay for this shit!"* He paced back and forth looking around for the shooters. *"I gotta to make it to Hound so I can get the ball rolling. Get this money flowing. The game don't stop for no one. Like PAC said , Never go to war until you get your money right."*

- - - - -

Paden sat in his car waiting on Santana to return. As his eyes were clued to Santana's car he didn't notice Carlos exiting the right side of his car with a 357 with a silencer in his hand as Shantez came from the back left hand side of the car aiming a 357 at him as well. Boxed in by both men, big Jimmy walked up to Paden's car door and aimed a pump right at Paden's head.

"Don't move!" Jimmy shouted in a low tone as Carlos and Shantez got into the back seat of Paden's car.

The investigator pissed himself at the sight of the double eyes pointed in his face. Jimmy opened the door of Paden's car and informed him to slide over. Jimmy took the wheel and fifteen minutes later they arrived at a small house in the middle of nowhere.

"Get out." Jimmy told Paden.

"Man what is this all about?"

"Shut the fuck up and keep moving." Jimmy swung the pump across the side of Paden's head. Paden grabbed the side of his head almost falling to the ground.

Jimmy then kicked him in the ass, "Keep moving." He guided Paden into the basement of the house and tied him up to a chair in the middle of the basement.

"Who do you work for?" Carlos asked staring Paden in the eyes that showed fear without question.

"I work for no one. I'm a private investigator." His voice shook.

"Who hired you to tail Sergeant Santana?" Carlos continued.

"Detective Hoffman." Paden said proudly hoping to save his own life.

"Where does he live?" Carlos asked

Even though Paden had been cooperative answering all of Carlos's questions, Gormez's men still carried out their orders. An order is an order. A slaughter is a slaughter. Working for the police department didn't save Detective Paden. The following night Hoffman found Paden's head on top of his fireplace.

Paula sat at a small desk in a master bedroom equipped with everything that she needed to make her stay comfortable at Gormez's lake house. Two bodyguards were posted outside her door for protection and to make sure she stayed put. During her two week stay she tried escaping but failed. Gormez made it perfectly clear that she will stay put until he talked to the other five families. He needed to find out why his family members were coming up dead. So this was for her own good.

Paula had one person on her mind and desperately wanted to get to him. She adored the way he smiled, talked, walked and just couldn't get him off her mind. She called Joey's phone once to hear his voice and to let him know she was out of town. She apologized for standing him up and promised to give him something special when she returned. But soon after that Gormez had his bodyguards confiscate her phone.

Paula moved from the desk over to the king sized bed and pressed the intercom button located on the night stand next to he bed. "Sara please bring me some orange juice." Two minutes later Sara knocked on the door.

"Come in."

"Hey sugar, how are you doing this afternoon."

Sara entered the bedroom and placed the tray with a glass of orange juice and a platter of crackers and cheese on the night stand.

"Sugar what's wrong?"

"Why does he always do this to me" Paula showed her

frustration with a grunt throwing her hands in the air.

"Calm down honey. Your uncle is only trying to protect you." She reached for Sara's hand to comfort her.

"I feel like I'm a prisoner."

"Paula it won't be long. You'll be back at home soon. You'll see." She ensured Paula with a gently loving pat on her hands. "Soon, honey soon." Sara got up from the bed and exited the room.

The bodyguard that stood guarding the door looked in on Paula to make sure she was still alive because they were not to trust anyone not even Sara, until Gormez found out what was going on.

- - - - -

Tony had met up with Mike's cousin Hound several days after the shoot out and gave him a sample of the pure heroin. Hound cut, bagged, and moved it for Tony because Tony was green when it came to the game. Tony watched Hound and learned a lot from him.

One day while posted up in a shooting gallery, (a place where fiends would shoot up) Tony watched Hound make transactions and watched the behavior of dope fiends. There was one in particular that stood out to him. A middle aged thick white woman with brown curly hair and a fat ass sat in the corner, on a nasty wore out couch nodding in and out like she was fighting her sleep. Her head nodding from side to side, as she almost fell off the couch she would catch herself. She'd briefly wake up, scratch her arm and ass.

Tony didn't know these were the real signs of an attic. "This is real life shit, not what's seen on TV. What is she doing in a place like this?"

Hound already knowing the white girl ignored Tony so that he could figure it out for himself. Tony walked over to the white girl and sparked a conversation.

"What's happening Snow White?"

The girl slowly looked up at Tony and leaned back as if she was getting ready to hit the flow but leaned in towards Tony,.

"Hey baby you got some work?"

"What you need?" Tony pulled out a five pack of crack cocaine.

"Mothafucker! I don't want no crack. You got some *boy*?"

Tony stood there shocked and didn't know what she was talking about.

"Yo Tony my man, that bitch want a fix. Some dope you know what I mean and she will do whatever you want for a cap." Hound yelled over to Tony.

"Follow me." Tony led the girl to a back room. Once in the back room Tony gave her a cap of heroin. She pulled out a top from a wine bottle. She poured the cap of heroine into the cap and mixed it with some spit. Then reached for her liter and placed the flame under the bottle top. She let the heroine heat to a bubble before grabbing a filter out the back of a loose cigarette and a needle that had dried up blood on it. She stuck the needle into the cap and drew the liquid in it. She rolled up her shirt sleeve to revealing existing track marks and sores all over. She began thumping her arm to find a vain.

"Shit!" She yelled pulling off her mini skirt and dusty panties that looked like they had never been washed.

She placed her two fingers between her pussy lips to spread one lip to the side. She inserted the needle into her pussy lip releasing the dope.

Tony was shocked out of his Ming. "Yo shorty what the hell you doing?"

The white woman smiled looking at Tony seductively. he sensed she was ready to fuck.

"I'm good shorty. That was on the house." And walked out of the room.


Hound was making a sells to a long line of customers. Tony smiled as Hound handed him five G's in less than an hour of hustling at the gallery.

# CHAPTER 15

Tyson, Joey, and Dantwan met back at the one bedroom house where they had the cocaine stashed. They needed to discuss current matters such as the missing half of bricks of cocaine and heroin. As the men sat at the round table Tyson led the conversation.

"Y'all already know the Mexicans are making noise and looking for the people who killed their people and robbed them, alright. It wont be long before they find out that it was us."

"How they gone know it was us?" Dantwan interrupted.

"Just listen nigga and learn something." Joey shushed Dee with a wave of his hand. And the men chuckled.

"Anyways as I told y'all before, the heroin would speak for itself. As of last week that dope hit the streets and every dope fiend in town is talking about it. Even the hustler's getting mad about the competition knocking their hustle. The streets are talking fellow and they are screaming Tony's name and some other dude name Hound. Tyson paused and scratched his head. I found out he's an old time big hat that got turned out on his own product."

"Aight Ty. What we need to do is run up on that nigga and touch him."

"Nah Dee. Listen to what I'm saying. Our luck has changed for the better. We ain't got to touch dude now. We in the clear baby! Tyson smirked, "Them Mexicans gone murk him for us."

"Wait what you getting at Ty, walk me through."

"Well, if the dope fiends and dealers know the dope on the streets the Mexicans do too. But if they don't we gone make sure they find out." Tyson rubbed his hands together with a smile on his face.

"Oh shit, yea I feel you man." Dantwan eyes lit up with excitement.

"One thing though we gotta make sure Tony doesn't get trapped and questioned. We can't have him telling where he got the dope." Joey chimed in but Tyson was one step ahead of him.

- - - - -

It had been two weeks since Reader had used drugs. She had gained a lil weight and her skin cleared. Reader stepped outside of her apartment in a brand new sweatsuit with a pair of white forces. She wore a diamond necklace with a medallion Jesus Christ on a cross with diamond chips throughout and two red ruby's in his eyes. hanging around her neck down to her breast.

Since the night of the shooting Reader realized how short life is and promised herself she wasn't smoking anymore crack. She wanted a better life for herself. Joey had always seen potential in Reader. He took her transformation serious and made her a lieutenant on the team. Most of the time she would be riding shotgun with him all over town, making pick ups and drop offs.

Reader stepped into the street feeling good and looking good. She was proud of the accomplishment to overcome drug addiction and getting money off what was killing her. She walked off the street in front of Jackie's apartment. She saw some young boys standing on the corner. Reader noticed Jackie walking down the street with Larry. Reader looked in their direction and yelled out,

"Yo Larry, let me holla at you for a minute."

Larry began walking across the street with Jackie riding his coat tail.

"What's happening Reader?"

"You got that ready?"

She fronted Larry some dope and wanted her money.

"Yeah I got that in the house. I'm ready for another round. Follow me to the house."

Reader and Jackie looked at each other and all three of them began walking towards Jackie's apartment. Reader and Jackie waited outside on the front porch while Larry went inside to get the money. He handed Reader 800 dollars and Jackie immediately thought about grabbing it but noticed the change in Reader's weight and clarity and just as quickly dismissed the thought. Which served her well because Reader has since been running every morning at Beck Middle School football field. And she knew that Reader had them hands long before drugs took her mind.

"Check this out lil sis. I'm about to put a down payment on this three bedroom house in Taylors. And as you can see I'm not fucked up no more so I'm coming to take my daughter off your hands. I hope you're cool with giving up Lorey."

Jackie took in Lorey for her big sister Reader, when Reader got turned out on crack by her ex boyfriend Willie, the same guy Reader chose over Chris and Joey in elementary school. Willie was a small time drug dealer that cheated on Reader with Jackie and also had a child with. Willie tried to turn Jackie out too but Jackie didn't fall victim to him like Reader did.

Jackie turned her back on Reader for leaving her responsible for Lorey when she was struggling to take care of her own child. Even though she was disappointed in her big sister deep down she still loved her and vice verse.

"I still love you Jackie and I appreciate you looking out for Lorey the best way you could. I'll be to get her in a few days." Reader handed Jackie 300 hundred dollars.

"Larry, I'll get at you in a few hours." Reader walked off Jackie's porch heading to the corner where the young boys stood selling crack and weed.

- - - - -

Detective Hoffman sat in his office, where he spent most of his time ever since he found Paden's head sitting on top of his fireplace. Hoffman became paranoid of everybody especially Santana. Santana would stare at him and make eye contact with a crooked smile that made Hoffman feel eerie. Hoffman began peeping out of windows, watching behind him, and carried three pistols. One in a holster, one in the ankle, and one in his back waist band.

Hoffman's case loads got backed up as he focused on the Chris Hill and Pedro case. He suspected the head on his fireplace was a direct connection, a threat that he was getting close to something. He decided to find out who the house belonged to that Chris was found dead in.

Hoffman grabbed his keys and half eaten sandwich off his desk and walked out the door keeping his eyes peered on his surroundings. Once in the parking lot Hoffman scurried to his unmarked car and locked the doors behind him. He scanned the parking lot to see if anybody was following him or watching him. But he didn't see that Santana was watching him from the window on the fifth flooring laughing.

- - - - -

Jesus Gormez sat around the round table in Las Vegas with five other drug lords from different states discussing the recent attacks on his family members. He wanted to know who was responsible.

"We have heard of your loses but it is neither family sitting here that's involved. We made a pact several years ago that our families should remain at peace and be allies ever since your family and the Garamond family went to war. So none of us broke the treaty my friend." Medal Gonzales spoke looking at the other leaders sitting around the table.

"Yes I understand that very clearly. But someone has taking hits out on me and my family."

"We sympathize with you. We will do our best to look into the matter to find out who's responsible. But keep in mind that we have our own families to worry about too." David Wright vowed, who held rank in North Carolina all the way to Washington.

"Keep doing what you're doing Jesus and we will help you find those responsible. I'll contact you in twelve hours." Vincent Perone who held a secret vendetta against the Gormez family. He walked away from the discussing with thinking this might be the perfect time to take over the Gormez's operation.

"Thank you Vincent and the rest of you. please tell your families i send my best wishes."

The men stood and shook hands . The men were escorted back to their limousines and left as Gormez stood behind for a few seconds to give orders to Shantez and Carlos. Before he got into his limousine he ordered them to contact his people on the streets to see if they heard anything about his heroin.

# CHAPTER 16

Across town, Green Avenue was on fire from rapid gunfire. Boom Boom Boom, Pop Pop Pop, Ra tat tat Ra tat tat,. People ran for conversation ducking behind cars and apartment buildings. Fiends running around like chickens with their heads cut off.

"Follow me!" Hound guided Tony as they were ducked behind a car with his weapon drawn ready to fire.

"Where them mothafuckers go?" Carlos yelled at his crew with A.K. 47 assault rifles drawn. "Check every damn apartment building and house around here! We're not leaving until we fine them." Shantez shouted.

Tony and Hound ran in an apartment through the back door and out the front then jumped into a candy red Tahoe that Tony bought from another drug dealer for fourteen thousand dollars just two hours ago. Tony crunk the car and took off like a bat out of hell. Coming out of the neighborhood towards the back end they ran into a road block set up by Gormez's men. They were checking cars that come through as if they were real police enforcements.

Tony reached under his seat and pulled out a mini sub machine gun with a reversible banana clip, holding a hundred round with exploding holo point bullets. He placed it into his lap with the barrel pointed out the driver side window. Slowing the car down and approaching the five Mexican men Tony told Hound, "Get ready." As he tapped the trigger with his finger.

Hound held his Mac Eleven with a reversible hundred round banana clip with info red beams attached. Gormez's men surrounded the vehicle two feet on all sides. Hound and Tony began letting off rounds after rounds, hitting three of the men killing them instantly while the other two men returned fire hitting hound in the arm.

Tony put the pedal to the metal taking off in a fish tail leaving a trail of smoke behind. A dozen men came out of nowhere firing their A.K. 47's putting holes in Tony's new truck,

"Mothafucker you're going to pay now!?

Fish tailing and took flight and cut two flips and smashed into a telephone pole then hitting a brick wall. Tony was thrown ten feet from the car but came back for Hound who was still in the car injured, his leg was trapped and he couldn't move.

"Keep it moving man. Go! Prepared to die he told Tony it was his time to meet Allah and with that said Tony left him to face his death. Gormez men ran up to the vehicle surrounding it with their weapons pointed at the car. Not knowing that Hound was prepared to die but vowed that he is going to take a few men with him.

Hound pretended to be dead peeping out of one eye while his finger hugged the trigger of his Mac Eleven. He waited for a few of the men to gather around the truck then he came alive blasting killing two men. Shantez creeped up on Hound from the opposite side of the truck with a  pump and let both barrels hit him in the face splashing Hound's brains all over the front interior.

"Where's the other one?" Shantez shouted.

"I don't know Sir." One of the men replied looking around in search for Tony.

"What do you mean you don't know?" Shantez shouted at the man. "What is your name?"

"Julio De Janero"

"How did you shoot it up? Show me how you did it." Shantez pointed his pump to the guys face. "Did you shoot the truck up like this." He squeezed the trigger putting the guys brains all over the street.

Carlos got on his phone to call Jimmy.

"Yea, Jim here."

"Send the clean up crew now."

No less than a few minutes two black vans with several men dressed in all black plastic suits began picking up the dead bodies and cleaning the blood off the street while another truck towed the wrecked truck to a junk yard to be crushed. The clean up crewed worked fast as sirens blared in the distance getting louder as they got closer to the scene.

"Hurry up boys the boys in blue will be here in a minute." Shantez looked at his watch.

"Just finished Sir." One of the men shouted.

"Okay lets get out of here." Carlos shouted as everybody jumped into their vans and cars leaving Green Avenue in the rear view mirror.

- - - - -

Paula was allowed to go back to her own house after Gormez heard back from the five families. He was told that their was not a hit on his family, just a robbery gone bad. Gormez knew that whoever pulled this off had to be smart and desperately wanted to find the son of a bitch.

Paula lost her job at the Citgo for failure to come to work. Gormez compensated her for her troubles and promised to talk to her manager. He also let a few things slip out of his mouth during Paula's stay. He blurted out in a heat of passions that Pedro's killer was a guy named Tony and that Tony took over a million dollars in cash. But the most shocking news that Paula overheard is that her families legacy is built off drugs and murders.

The first thing Paula did when she settled in was to call Joey. She had missed his voice and sense of humor plus she wanted to take her mind off her uncle's deceiving ways.

"Hey babygirl."

"How you know it was me?" She smiled

"Caller I.D baby." Joey laughed.

"Oh so you've saved my number name and number."

"True."

"So what you doing tonight?"

"Whatever you want to do."

"I want you to come over and keep me company."

"Aight I can do that but right now I'm handling business."

"Then what's time will you be able to come by."

"Give me a couple of hours." Joey waved his hand at Dantwan to keep the noise down.

"Ok baby, I'll see you then."

Paula laid back on her bed thinking about how she was going to put it on Joey when he came over as her phone began ringing.

"Hello."

"I just realized I don't have your address." They both laughed.

"Oh yea I'll share my location." She texted Joey her location as she continued to lay on her bed. She drifted into thoughts of her families trouble and the name Tony. She didn't know this Tony but she instantly hated him for killing her Pedro. She also remembered Joey and that lady talked about a guy with the same thing and wondered if this could be the same Tony.

Paula brushed the thoughts out of her mind and rose to take a hot shower to prepare for her night with Joey. She stripped down to her birthday suit and slid into her bath filled with warm water and coconut oil and lavender bath salt to relax.

- - - - -

Joey hung up with Paula and turned his attention back to the family meeting. As Tyson began speaking again, Dantwan's phone began ringing.

"Yea tell it."

"Hey baby you still mad at me." Lisa whined like a little puppy.

"This is not a good time Lisa. I'll call you back."

"Aye listen that boy that took that shit out of here just came banging on my door. Scared and out of breath."

"Say what!"

"Hold on for a second." Dantwan began telling Tyson and Joey what Lisa had just told him. This nigga got some big balls.

"Hand me the phone." Tyson reached for Dantwan's phone. "Lisa this Ty, tell me about that nigga Tony and what just happened." Lisa told Ty everything before Ty gave the phone back to Dantwan.

Dantwan made his conversation short with Lisa. He was still sore about how she let Tony in her house giving him the opportunity to steal his dope. So when she asked if he was coming over he blurted out in frustration he'd see her later and hung up the phone.

"Well, boys there is our answer to Joey's question. Tyson smirked with a devilish grin.

"What are you talking about?" Dantwan asked.

"Well as we just heard, Tony is a man on the run. Now if we can find him you can get your payback and that will put us in the clear. Once the police find his body and the investigation stops there.

"Thats not going to work. That's only going to put us back at square one." Joey added.

"What you thinking about Joey because it sounds good to me." Dantwan agreed with Tyson's plan. He wanted Tony's head on a platter.

"We'll still be sitting on a brick of pure heroin once Tony is dead."

"I am right with you Red and I got a plan for that but neither one of you need to know everything right now."

They looked at Tyson like he said something wrong. So Ty had to convince them,

"Trust me boys. I got us covered."

They trusted Ty to handle business. They ended the family meeting and stood to leave. Each one giving the other around and a hug as they walked out the side door of the house.

# CHAPTER 17

Larry was sitting on Jackie's back porch making a crack sell to a fiend when out of nowhere Tony was standing beside him with a baby submachine, breathing hard and sweating.

"Who's in the house?"

"Man what's up. I am going to get you your money, just give me some time, please man!" Scared out of his mind.

"I got a deal for you that will wipe the slat clean. But we got to discuss this inside."

"Ok let's go." Larry opened the screen door and allowed Tony inside Jackie's apartment. Tony walked into the apartment and headed straight to the windows to check the streets and surroundings with the submachine raised up to his face looking like KRS one on the Boogie Down Production Album Cover, "Criminal Minded."

"Man what's the deal?"

"Check this out, we can kill that bill if you let me chill here for a minute or two." Tony stated trying to catch his breath and collect his thoughts. "Is anybody else here with you?" Looking around paranoid.

"Nah Jackie and the children went somewhere. They can be

back anytime now."

"Well I need you to do one thing for me."

"And what's that?" Larry now knew that his debt would be cleared for sure.

"I need you to find me a ride and I got half an ounce for you." Tony stood still looking out the window and checking his clip in his gun.

"For real!" Excited at the thought of a half ounce for getting Tony a simple ride.

"Straight up do, just find me a ride and I'mma look all the way out for you."

"Aight, I'll be right back."

"Hold up man don't tell nobody that you seen me, ok."

"I got you man." Larry walked out of the apartment through the back door.

- - - - -

Reader was standing on the block when she noticed Larry walking up the street in a hurry. She called out to Larry. Larry came running across the street to Reader.

"What's up Reader."

"I got something for you. I'mma bless you so you can get on your feet."

"That's mad love but right now I'm about to make an easy come up off this busta ass Tony."

"You talking about Tony that left his boy Mike to be killed by them jack boys." She threw the blame on them to steer it away from Joey and his crew. But Larry didn't buy it.

"Reader you know just as well as i know that them jack boys didn't have shit to do with killing Mike. We saw you looking out your window the same time we looked at out of Jackie"s."

"Anyway how you gone come up off that nigga." They say he's in hiding.

"Yea he's in hiding alright, hiding in your sister's apartment. He said if I get him a ride he gone give me an eight ball of crack so you know I'm game for that."

"Boy is you crazy. You helping the nigga that almost killed you a couple weeks ago."

- - - - -

Ever since Tony and Mike damn near killed Larry he had moments of revengeful thoughts on his mind. Reader had him thinking that time is now.

"You right Reader what you think I should do?"

"Hold up for a second while I make a phone call."

"What's happening Reader." Joey answered the phone as he drove down Laurens road, headed into Mauldin, South Carolina.

"Ya boy Tony, I know where he at right now."

"Hold that thought Reader."

Joey grabbed his other cell phone sitting on the passenger seat. He dialed Tyson's number and gave him the update. Tyson then dialed Dantwans to do the same. Joey made U-turn headed back to Greenville.

"Where he at?" Joey asked Reader.

"You wont believe it if i told you." She laughed. "Just come over to my old apartment."

Joey put the other phone to his mouth again. "Meet me in the bricks."

Twenty minutes later Joey, Tyson and Dantwan met Reader and Larry behind Readers old apartment building. Larry told them what tony wanted him to do. Joey lost his train of thought for a split second, I'm plotting with the nigga who took my girl.

"Larry I want you to get in the van with me. I'll be the ride you came up with. Let Tony know that all I asked for was a crack." Tyson gave Larry his role then turned to Dee and Joey. "I want y'all to get in the back of the van under the blankets."

The men agreed as Tyson gave Reader her role. "Reader when I pull up in front of Jackies apartment you run to the van like you're trying to sell me som crack. If Tony is paranoid like Larry says he is then he'll be very impatient and push his way into the van.

"Tony strapped with a submachine too." Larry informed.

"Aight. So as I was saying, once I turn on the radio and flip through the stations, y'all will spring into action like the friendly neighborhood Spider-Man. Everybody got it?"

Everybody nodded their heads in unison.

"Hold up what I'm getting out of the deal." Larry asked in greed.

Joey disliking Larry knew exactly what he was going to do to Larry. "I got him."

"Ok. Everybody let's do this." Tyson instructed.

- - - - -

Karen was pushing A.J. in his wheelchair coming out of the Motel Six off old Augusta road, when they noticed a police cruiser parked across the street with two white officers getting out of the car.

"Damn here come them fuck boys, always fucking with a nigga. You aint dirty is you?" A.J. asked Karen. She shook her head no to indicate she was clean except for old warrants.

The officers approached them.

"Excuse me would you be Andre Johnson. Looking at A.J.

"Yes Sir what have I done now?"

"You're under arrest for the murder of a one Michael Wilson." The chubby officer stated as Karens mouth dropped wide open in shock.

"Baby call my peeps and let them know what's going on."

"I got you baby." Karen watched the officers handcuff him while tears rolled down her cheeks. The officers pushed A.J. To their cruiser then placed him in the back seat as they put his wheelchair in the trunk before hauling him off to jail. Karen got into her baby blue Cadi and called Lisa.

"Hello."

"They just took A.J to jail for murder. Karen yelled as she changed lanes coming up Old Augusta road, passing club 327.

"Say what."

Karen explained what happened before Lisa made a phone call to Dantwan. After Lisa and Karen had their heart to heart a few weeks ago, Karen decided to give A.J. A chance. She opened her heart up to him. The two became inseparable. She even helped him make his rounds and made a couple of hand sells for him.

Karen felt they had a lot in common. They liked the same movies, video games, foods..etc. A.J. even took her to meet his mother, even though his moma the type that will tell his business. She'd be quick to tell Karen about his other women so he made sure they didn't talk long and that he was present. He even trusted Karen with his dope and money. They had plans to get an apartment together off white horse road. Karen drove down Old Augusta Road passing long john silver coming up on Church street. I'm with you baby. You don't have to worry.

- - - - -

Jesus Gormez paced back and forth across the carpet cussing and fussing at Shantez, Carlos, and Jimmy about their fuck up.

"You must be a complete moron. You lost Tony and you killed one of your men in front of your other men. You imbecile."

"Sir we will find him. He cant hide from us." Shantez tried to calm Jesus. My man failed his duties and therefor I took the proper action to assure no one else screws up, Sir.

"Oh is that right. Since we don't want no more screw ups and we're taking action, put your left hand on this stump." Gormez took the axe that Jimmy handed him.

"Sir this is not necessary. I will personally catch this Tony guy."

"Did you think twice about the young man's life you took about his screw up? Now put your hand on the chopping block."

Gormez yelled.

Jimmy grabbed Shantez by the back of the neck before he could take another step. Carlos joined in to assist Jimmy making Shantez put his left hand on the tree stump.

"Please sir you don't have to do this."

Gormez raised the ax and came down hard on Shantez's left hand chopping it off at the bone. Shantez screamed then fainted. And the men begin to laugh.

# CHAPTER 18

Larry jumped out of the passenger side of the van and ran up to Jackie's front porch. Tony was watching though the cracked widow. As soon as Larry went into the house Tony checked his clip in his gun, "What's up nigga. Damn I thought you jetted on me."

"Nah nigga you know how hard it is to find a ride, if you aint got no hard on you .

"Is that my ride outta here?" Tony peeped out the window.

"Yea that's your ride but my man want a hit of crack and he will take you to hell and back if you want him to."

Tony peeped out the window again to check his surroundings before exiting out the door.

"Aye can I get that half of ounce now, nigga?" Larry stopped Tony in his tracks.

"Oh yeah I almost forgot. Tony reached into his pants pulling out an ounce of cocaine and broke it in half. He tossed the half to Larry as he opened the front door and took one last look around. He took off running towards the van and jumped into the passenger seat. As soon as he got into the van Reader ran up to the driver side,

"What's up Bob what you need, I got what you want." Showing him two cracks in her hand.

Tony being anxious and ready to go treated Reader no different that the other crack heads he deal with,

"Bitch get the fuck away from this van with that fake shit."

Reader looked at Tyson, then stuck her middle finger up at Tony and walked off in the opposite direction.

"Where to partner?" Tyson asked as Tony looked around the van at the boxes and blankets spread about.

"Just drive, nigga." Tony repositioned the side mirror to see if they were being followed.

"Your boy tell you what I want right?"

"Yea I got you. Just drive." Tony pulls out the half ounce and broke of a hundred dollar piece and handed it to Tyson.

"That ought to take care of you for a minute."

Tony put his gun on the floor as they left out of Fieldcrest community heading towards Nichol Town community. So Tyson thinking now is the perfect opportunity to reach for the stereo button to turn on the radio to get things poppin' off. But all of a sudden Dantwan's cell phone began ringing.

- - - - -

Jackie was getting out an unmarked police car two streets over from Fieldcrest apartments. She made a visit to the police station to give information to Sergeant Santana about that murder of Mike Wilson and identified Joey and A.J. She hated Joey and wanted to see him go down so she did what she thought she had to do to get back at him. Jackie didn't want to be seen getting out of the unmarked car so she walked back to Fieldcrest. She spotted the dusty van and locked eyes with Tyson as he passed by her but didn't think anything of it.

She continued on her walk. I am a snitch bitch." She began laughing and prancing down the street proud of herself. Shortly after she seen Reader and Larry standing in between her building talking and ducked behind the dumpster to listen in on their conversation.

"Look nigga, if Jackie knew you had that nigga in her house you know that bitch would cut a fool. So you better take this and shut the fuck up."

"Damn Reader, I thought you said you were going to bless me. What the fuck I'mma do with a five pack."

"Nigga, you already got an eight ball." Reader let out a sigh as she realized that she would soon have to cut Larry off completely. His greed would get the best of him and she'd have to have Joey them merk his ass. As Larry continued to beg for a bigger handout they heard bottles rattling behind the dumpster.

"Who is that over there?" Larry called out but didn't get an answer.

So Reader pulled out her 38 handgun and cocked it. "I bet if I send six slugs over there you'll respond then. Show yo'self."

Jackie came from behind the dumpster raising hell, "What nigga been in my house?" Placing her hands on her hip letting them know she heard them and wanted an answer.

"Oh boy here we go." Larry knew he was in trouble with his lady.

Reader began to laugh as she put her gun behind her back in her waist line.

"Damn right here we go."

"Wait a minute! Where the fuck you been? And where are the kids?" Larry turned the conversation around.

Jackie explained that her friend girl was watching the kids while she made some runs across town to pay bills. Reader knew that Jackie was living but Larry ate it up like a slice of pizza.

"Alright y'all I'm out. Jackie I'll come pick up Lorey tomorrow as soon as they deliver my bedroom and living room suit.

Jackie and Larry headed towards her apartment arguing.

- - - - -

A.J. was summoned from his cell by Detective Hoffman. Two police officers escorted A.J. to Hoffman's office with A.J. handcuffed to his wheelchair.

"How are you doing Mr. Johnson?" Hoffman looking at paper work that scattered across his desk.

"I'm good."

"Well I'll get straight to it. We have a witness linking you to the murder of a one Mike Johnson. You've been identified as the shooter. Hoffman looking A.J. in the eyes and watching his body movements.

"Sir, I'mma be real with you. I was in the area standing on the blocks when shots fired. I tried to make it behind a car and didn't make it, that's how I got hit. If I knew anything more I'd tell you. But I'm not your guy. I've never been arrested or in any type of trouble before except when I was twelve and got caught trashing the school on the last day of school as a joke."

Hoffman watched A.J.'s demeanor as he explained his story. A.J. stared him straight in the eyes without wavering or stuttering. Hoffman believed everything A.J. said simply because the paperwork corroborated it too.

"Okay Johnson. Do you know a Joey Williams.

"Yeah what did he do?"

"He's a person of interest for this same murder. How do you suppose that is?"

A.J. laughed at the accusation. but he knew that someone saw them and that someone was talking.

"Get out of here. Joey with a gun. Joey as a killer. Nah no way. He ain't got a killer bone in his body, he might even be scared of guns."

"How you know?"

"Because shit, his old lady be whooping his ass." A.J. made a joke causing Hoffman to join on in laughter.

"Do you know a Jackie Tucker?" Hoffman asked while shuffling papers on his desk. It's unknown if he intentionally allowed A.J. to see the signed statement with Jackie's name on it or if he thought since A.J. was in a wheelchair he couldn't see across his desk but he did.

"Hell yea! Who don't know drama queen. That's the one that keeps her foot in Joey's ass." He punch a big whole in Jackie's statement with the one statement.

"Wait! So you're saying that Joey and Jackie Tucker are a couple?"

"They recently broke up bout a week ago. He's dating some classy girl now. Jackie been causing problems between them ever since. You know how girls do."

"Ah I see now."

"Ok Johnson, the magistrate will set you a bond but since you've been cooperative with me Ill ask that you be allowed to sign your own recognizance, alright?"

"Thank you Sir.

Hoffman's two officers escorted A.J. back to his cell. Hoffman pondered about the case for a few minutes. That damn bitch trying to fuck up that young boys life because he don't want her anymore, damn shame. He picked up his phone calling Sergeant Santana who was dropping Jackie off at her destination.

- - - - -

Beep Beep Beep! Dantwan's cell phone began ringing over the radio.

"What the fuck was that?" Tony yelled looking in the back of the van.

"Oh that's my cell phone."

"Man you the police or something?" Paranoid out of his mind.

"Chill homie, ain't nobody the police."

Tony reached down on the floor in search of his gun which was now in Joey's possession. Tony realizing that his gun was now gone. He knew he was setup and needed to escape the van. He reached for the door handle to make a jump for it. He rubbed all over the vans passenger door only to find that the latch was missing. He turned to Tyson in rage and fear ready to attack but was faced with two 45 handguns pointed at his head, held by Joey and Dantwan.

"I told you to chill homie."

Dantwan slapped him across the face then snatched him into the back of the van. The next slap rendered him unconscious. Dantwan then grabbed his phone off his hip,

"I told you I'll be by there later. Stop blowing up my damn phone Lisa."

- - - - -

Twenty minutes later Tyson pulled the van up to the shooting gallery across town on Anderson road. Tyson got out of the van leaving the other behind. Five minutes later he returned as all of the dope fiends were leaving out of the house. He had paid the house a thousand dollars to leave for the night.

"Bring him inside."

125

Dantwan and Joey guided Tony inside the house. They ducked taped him to a chair that sat in one of the back bedrooms. Dantwan had a field day slapping Tony around and pouring cold water on him to wake him up when he pasted out. Every time Tony opened his eyes he was faced with Dantwan smiling at him with a mouth full of diamonds and gold plated teeth and a 45 in his hand.

"How you doing Tony?" Tyson asked.

"Come on man, it aint got to be like this. I'll pay you man."

"Dog we didn't kill you. You killed yourself with that dumb stunt you pulled." Tyson walked closer to Tony as Dantwan's phone began to ring yet again.

"What the fuck is it!"

"Nigga don't be yelling at me. I'm just calling to let you know that the police got A.J."

"For what?"

"Karen said for the murder of somebody name Mike Wilson."

"Alright babygirl. If anything else happens keep me posted." His attitude lightened towards Lisa.

"Ok baby I love you."

Dantwan called Ty and Joey into another room to let them know what happened to A.J.

Then men went back to where Tony was tied up. Tyson had a quick conversation with Tony.

" Ok Tony today might be your lucky day."

"Ok man. Anything you want just ask."

"We need to know where you stashed the heroin and the money you made."

"I sold most of it but I have about three ounces put up and two hundred thousand to go along with it."

"Where you put it Tony?"

"I got the three ounces on me. I can take you to the money."

Tony snapped his finger which was queue for Dantwan who approached Tony and slapped the shit out of him with his 45. He grabbed the bag of crack from his pants along with some crack.

"Where is the money?" Tony continued as Tony started to stutter causing Dantwan to hit him again.

"I am going to ask one more time? Where is the fucking money?"

"At my mom's house."

"Where she live?" Tony hesitated again and Dantwan put steel to head slapping him once again.

"On Elder Street in Nicholtown. The pink house on the right. Buried under a brick in the back yard next to a rusty bike." Tony feeling weaker and weaker from heavy amounts of blood lost.

"Tony if we find the money, you'll live. If not you will die a slow death, understood?"

"Joey call them boys to go check."

Joey walked into another room and called Reader. He explained what he wanted her to do and to contact him immediately once she got the money in her hands. Then called Paula to let her know he would be a little late coming over. She made him feel guilty for being later but he promised to make it up to her. Joey disconnected the call as he went into the other room with his crew to find Dantwan standing over Tony, repeatedly slapping the shit out of him while Tyson was in the corner cooking up a hot shot of pure dope.

Twenty minutes later Joeys phone rung with Reader on the other end.

"Everything is everything."

"The bank cleared the check." Joey announced to his boys.

# CHAPTER 19

"Sir just a couple more days and we will have Mr. Jesus Gormez right where we want him. Then we can go to the US Attorneys General with enough evidence to indict the bastard. Federal Agent Johnson A.K.A Sergeant Santana tried to convince the US secretary of Defense Agent Williams, for more time.

"I hope you're right Johnson. As I recall it took my skills to track down Casper A.K.A Rico Riley who you gave up on.

"Yea I remember. This time is different though. If I don't contact you back in 48 hours send he troops in."

"Aye, be sure to let Hoffman know you're on the right side of this so he doesn't become a problem with this investigation."

Williams was a brilliant agent. He was promoted and giving a Medal of Honor for binging down one of America's most dangerous criminals.

"Yes Sir."

- - - - -

A.J.'s bail was posted at one hundred thousand dollars. The female Judge he faced denied him the chance to sign his own reconnaissance due to the nature of the crime and A.J. Was escorted back to his cell.

He proceeded to the phones that hung in the bull pen of the jail. After the operator gave her spill about three way calling and time limits his call was connected.

"Hey baby." Karen was excited to hear from A.J.

"What going on Boo?"

"What you need me to do?"

"My bond one hundred thousand. Fine me a bondsman fast and the get the money from Dantwan and come get me out of here."

"Lisa already called Dantwan but we're waiting on his to call back."

A.J. Noticed two familiar faces looking at him so he got off the phone with Karen. "Ok babygirl, call him back and see what's up. I'll call you back in an hour."

"Ok I love you."

A.J. Adjusted his wheelchair breaks and rolled himself back to his cell. Followed by the boys staring at him.

"What's up A.J. One of the young boys named Mark Wilson who was Mike Wilson's little brother.

A.J. recognized Mark's face and immediately knew there was going to be a problem. and he was in no position to fight off any attacks on his life being confined to a wheelchair.

"Yo Mark. That some fucked up shit y'all doing running around here telling the police I had something to do with your brothers murder."

"Look man the streets are talking."

"That's not what the police just told me." Hoping the young boy was as stupid as his dead brother.

"What the pigs say?"

"Hoffman told me that they were looking for some guy name Tony and Horse or Hound for your brothers death. They got me in here to get information. A.J. Only knew about Tony and Hound from the APB put out by Tyson.

Marks took back on the wall and began thinking because he had his ear to the streets and heard that Tony and Hound been running the streets since his brother's death. Damn did they kill my brother.

"Man I believe that Tony set your brother up to take a fall for a lick that Tony and Hound pulled. That's what the streets saying."

Mark stared at A.J. lost in thought. "Aight I'll holla at you later." And walked out of his cell straight to make a phone call. It took an hour worth of collect calls for Mark to track down the truth. And they planned on servicing A.J. Ass when he came into the bullpen open ward.

A few minutes later A.J. came out of his cell and entered the open ward bullpen. He turned his head and looked at Mark and his home boy and noticed they were mean mugging him. A.J. knew that the shit was about to hit the fan. Mark and his partner began moving slowly in his direction trying not to be noticed and trying to conceal the weapon Mark was holding. But A.J. spotted the ice pick. And just as they were 5 feet away from A.J. a guard called out for him.

"Andre Johnson."

"Yea that's me!" A.J. yelled out to get the officer to turn in his direction.

"You're outta here. So pack your things."

A.J. Cut his loses. They can have that shit.

"I don't have nothing, you can take me now."

The officer came to get A.J. and rolled him out the ward. A.J. looked back at Mark and his homie with a smile on his face.

- - - - -

"Come on man, you said you was going to let me go free." Tony pleaded crying real tears.

The only freedom for a man is when he has nothing else to lose." Tyson told Tony.

Joey handed Tyson the dirty syringe filled with a hot shot of pure dope. Tony tried to put up a fight but the ropes were too tight. Dantwan slapped Tony in the mouth with his 45 handgun to calm him down. Ty grabbed Tonys right arm and inserted the syringe.

"Y'all go ahead and wipe down the room and everything we touched. " Tyson ordered as the drugs started to take affect. Tony began laughing and talking sluggish. He could barely hold his head up and his eyes rolled to the back of his head. Soon after he started foaming at the mouth and went into convulsion. When he stopped Ty went over and placed two fingers to his neck to check his pulse and noticed his pulse was very slow. So he knew Tony would be gone in about 2 more minutes.

"Joey you got that glock nine?" Tony wiped off the syring and placed it in Tony's hand.

"Yeah I got it." Joey dug in a black bag pulling out the gun that they used to kill Chris Hill and Pedro Gormez. Then pulled out the other gun that was used to kill Mike.

Joey wiped the guns down then handed it to Tyson. Tyson one by one placed the gun in Tony's hand for fingerprints then tossed the guns into an clean empty bag. Tyson look around the room making sure everything was clean. The Joey remembered they had the 44 magnum and twenty five automatic that was used to kill Julio and Papi at Timothy Park.

"Hurry up with the fingerprints so we can get to his moma's house." Tyson ordered and the three men left in the van.

Twenty minutes later they arrived in Nicholtown Community and road down Rebecca Street and made a left turn on Elder Street. They parked the van at the bottom of Elder Street so they could walk the rest of the way. When they reached Tony's mom's house the porch light was on. Tyson removed the back pack from his arm and handed it to Dantwan. Dantwan walked to the back of the house and crawled under the house and began dumping the weapons out.

Once the men gathered back into the van Dantwan sighed in relief, "It's done." Smiling showing his gold fronts. Then they dropped Joey off at his friends car that he borrowed. And Dantwan was dropped off in Roosevelt Apartments at Lisa's place while Tyson headed home to Tonya.

- - - - -

Joey went to Fieldcrest and pulled into the block where Reader was standing in an all red track suit with matching shoes and hat. She was talking to a couple of hustlers as Joey pulled up beside her. Damn she looking good.

"What's happening babygirl?"

"Waiting on you baby boy." Reader walked towards the car swinging her hips that seemed to be getting thicker by the day.

As Reader got into the passenger seat Jackie appeared out of nowhere calling Joey's name.

"Yea what's up Jackie?"

"Can you give me a ride to the store?"

Jackie didn't have to go to the store. She just hated seeing Reader and Joey together lie they were a couple. She used to think they were fucking behind her back back in the day. And now that Reader was getting herself together those same thoughts came creeping back into her head.

"Get in."

Jackie hoped in the back seat. Joey drove to Citgo where Paula use to work at and noticed a white limousine parked it front.Jackie got out of the car first to enter the store. She saw two men holding the manager up by his collar and slapping him around. They heard the store bell ring indicating someone entered the store and looked at Jackie.

"My bad, and none of my business." Jackie turned around and walked back out of the store running to the car. "Let's try another store."

"Why Jackie, I got business to handle?"

Jackie told him what he saw in the store. And he agreed to drive her to another store. He didn't know it at the time that it was Carlos and Jimmy were the ones in the store slapping the manager around.

"Before we go the next store, I have a stop to make. Joey looked to his right. Where to Reader?"

Reader gave Joey the directions to where she had hid the money he had her pick up.

Once Reader brought the bag to the car, Joey unzipped the bag to check it then tried to zip it quickly to avoid Jackie from seeing. But she already saw it and knew she was missing out on his new come up.

Joey took Jackie to the store then dropped them both off in the court where Jackie lived.

"Joey how long you gone keep treating me like this?"

"What the hell you talking about Jackie?"

"Stop all the games Joey."

Joey bust out in laughter as if he had been watching Martin Lawrence kick Pam out and no matter how many times he did it each time was funnier than the last.

"Get out this car Jackie."

I'm serious Joey. I only had that nigga in my house to make you jealous. You know that."

"What we had is over. Ain't no need going back to the pass. I allowed you so much room and all you ever did was abuse me. I'm no good to you now."

"Fuck you Joey. You make me sick." She slammed the car door.

Joey sped off leaving her standing there watching him leave. Joey then stopped the car and back it up to Jackie.

"Jackie."

She turned around smiling thinking he had changed his mind and wanted to confess his love for her. Boy was she wrong. Joey stared at her for a brief moment then started laughing in her face as he pulled off leaving her and their pass in the wind.

# CHAPTER 20

Dantwan noticed A.J.'s brand new baby blue lac sitting on twenty two's as he walked up to Lisa's door. As soon as he knocked Lisa opened the door.

"Hey baby." She was excited to see him.

"Where you going?"

"Just going to A.J.'s car for him. He's in the house."

"I thought you said he was in jail." Ready to give her another ass whooping if she was living to him.

"He was but Karen posted his bond." She grabbed Dantwan's hand that was reaching to strike her if she was lying to him again. "Let's me get this stuff for him. Go ahead on in. I'll be right back."

She walked fast down the steps to A.J.'s car.

"Hurry up." He waited for her at the front door instead of going inside. When she came back up the steps they both stepped inside her apartment.

"We need to talk and we need to talk now, my nigga." A.J. sat in his wheelchair near the couch.

Dantwan walked over to him and grabbed the handle bars of his wheelchair and pushing him into Lisa's bedroom. Once inside A.J. explained everything that happened in jail and at the police station. Dantwan assured A.J. that everything had been taking care of and that he'll reimburse Karen the money she spent for his bond.

Ten minutes later they went back into the living room to join Lisa and Karen who were sitting on the couch talking. They sat around drinking and smoking weed until Lisa pulled Dantwan into her bedroom where they laid up the entire night. A.J. and Karen stayed up watching late night comedy shows, hugging, followed by oral sex until they finally fell asleep around 5a.m.

- - - - -

Santana met with Carlos and Jimmy at the Haywood mall agin. A special meeting was called and Santana took this opportunities to wear a wire to collect evidence. He also had over sixty federal agents on stand by watching his every move. After his first meeting behind the Gap store with Mr. Gormez, Santana advised the surveillance team to setup surveillance inside the Gap store. Santana was ready to get this job over with and all he needed was some concrete evidence and he felt that today was the day.

Santana followed Jimmy and Carlos to the same area in the shaft tunnels. But was confused when they passed by the back entrance of the Gap store and into the Dillards back entrance. Damn! Slick Mothafucker. He didn't see that coming

Once inside the Dillard's store they went into another office with three different rooms. Then they escorted Santana through the second door on the right that led to a garage where a black van with tinted windows was sitting idle.

"Get in Santana." Jimmy ordered as he shoved him into the van.

Santana knew then that something was wrong. He reached into his coat pocket and pressed his distress gps locator button to alarm the sixty federal agents that he was in trouble. But little did he know Gormez was several steps ahead of him. The radar blocker installed in the van blocks all radar signals. Santana kept pressing the button like he was on a game show. Pressed and looked but no agents came to his rescue and he panicked as the four men stared at him and the van took off.

"Where are we going?" Ready to try his hand at taking on all four men by himself until he felt a gun shoved into his ribs.

"Don't worry about it, you'll find out when we get there." Carlos tapped the back of the drivers seat signaling him to keep ahead.

Thirty minutes later they arrived at their destination. The double doors opened and Santana was shoved out fo the van on to gravel.

"Whats's up with all the shoving dude."

Jimmy pushed him again causing Santana's head to jerk hard. Santana rubbed his neck, "Shit!"

Jimmy pushed him again to keep Santana moving forward. Push after push got Santana closer to the end of a mountain cliff where Gormez stood in an all white tailored suit with matching white gators and an all white fedora hat with a pink feather tucked on the side. To his right and left side stood two twin white pit bulls with pink noses. Gormez stared Santana in his eyes,

"I am glad you could make it Sergeant Santana or should I say Federal Agent Johnson."

As Johnson looked around for an escape route, ready to take off just as he felt a sharp pain and total darkness with white spots due to a blow in the head from the butt of a pump from Carlos. Blood oozed out of his head while he was out cold.

- - - - -

Joey knocked on three doors before he found Paula's house. He tried to think of a lie to give her as to why he was an hour and half late. Paula answered the door on his third knock, "Hey Sweetie. what took you so long?"

Joey entered into her house eyeing the surrounding. "Car trouble."

Paula laughed at his lie, "Really." She paused, "Well have you ate Mr. Car trouble. I'd hate for the dinner I prepared for us to go to waste."

"I'm starving baby." Thinking more about the seafood between her legs than the plate.

After dinner they gathered onto her black leather sofa and got comfortable.

"How was your day, Joey."

"Too long." Joey rubbed the back of his neck.

"So what kind of job got you stressed?"

Silence struck Joey. He wasn't sure if now is the right time to tell Paula about his work.

"I'm going to tell you the truth. I hustle baby. But listen I plan on getting out the game real soon because I want us to bloom together like roses in the Spring time."

"Boy please don't even try to come up in here and try to run game on me." She laughed causing Joey to laugh too.

Paula grabbed Joey roughly by the collar pulling him close to her. She planted one of most moist seductive kissed on his lips that Joey had ever encountered. One thing led to another as they aggressively undressed each other. Paula licked and bit all around Joey's nipples as she unbuckled his belt and let his pants fall to the floor. She stuck her tongue into his mouth and he began sucking it then turned Paula around and began licking on her neck down to the arch of her back. Chills ran through Paula's body as instant wetness flowed between her legs. Joey bent Paula over on the couch as she spread her legs allowing Joey easy access. he grabbed bot of her ass checks and pushed them up, spreading them as he entered her sweet spot from behind.

"Ooh baby." Paula moaned feeling his pipe thrust her insides.

Joey began grinding slow and smooth enjoying the tightness of her walls gripping his pipe.

"Ooh baby dont' stop." She moaned louder as she thrust her ass back at him. "Just like that." As Joey stroked faster and harder.

Joey's penis got harder and he went faster hitting her Gspot. She got wetter with every stroke and just as her breathing became heavy Joey knew she was reaching climax so he hit her G-spot spot hard then grinning on it as her body began to shake and she screamed,

"Yea that's it baby, it's coming Papi."

Joey snatched his dick out, flipped her over , and put her legs over his shoulders. He went down licking and sucking her clit. Paula began thrusting her hips towards him as her climax was about to erupt just as Joey stopped abruptly then stuck his dick into her beating fast and hard.

"I'm cumming baby. I'm cumming!" Paula and Joey both screamed in ecstasy. Both rolling their hips in unison as they kissed each other and there breathing slowed, sweating like wild hogs in a fight.

Joey grabbed Paula picking her up and carried her to the bedroom where they cuddled breathless and sweaty. Once Paula caught her breath she went to the bathroom to grab a wash cloth. She washed herself in the sink then grabbed another wash cloth and took it to the bedroom to wash Joey off with it. As she walked into the bedroom she flipped the light switch and began washing Joey. While she washed Joey he looked around her room. Noticing a photo on her nightstand with her and a Mexican guy that looked familiar to him.

"Who is that guy in the picture with you, a boyfriend?"

"That's my cousin Pedro. He was killed a bout a month ago."

Paula noticed Joeys eyes got wide at that moment.

- - - - -

Agent Johnson was awaken by the sound of a loud horn sounding from a tub boat that was two hundred yards out to sea. Johnson was hogged tied and hanging from a rope over the ocean from a large fishing rail. Opening his eyes wider to focus his vision he saw Gormez, Carlos, Jimmy and Shantez (who had bandages wrapped around his left hand), standing on the deck of the boat. Shantez was pointing out at the ocean at a chocolate of sharks approaching. Gormez and his men began walking from the higher boat deck to the bottom deck. Gormez called for one of the men to come with the snap of his finger. The old man aged around 65 skinny with a white beard and bronze complexion followed Gormez's order.

"Captain feed the babies." Gormez blew snark from his cigar that hung from the corner of his mouth.

The captain began throwing bloody fish into the ocean as the sharks of all sizes devoured the fish. Johnson hung right about the school of sharks as he counted at least six man eating sharks surrounding him.

"How was your nap Agent Johnson?"

Johnson hung like a black slave on a tree.

"I've had better days."

Johnson had a nonchalant attitude. No need in showing any emotion now. His death was seconds away and he made peace with that.

"Tell me agent. Who can get you off the hook no?"

Gormez men began laughing at his sense of humor.

"I guess you're wondering where's your back up?"

Gormez held up Santana's tracking device in the air.

"Yea we found this on you while you were knocked out."

Santana's transmitter gave Johnson's location when they took him out of the van. And the federal agents sprung into action. But by the time they reached the top of the mountain Santana had been moved out to sea.

"Thanks to my inside man Christopher Hoffman, who found out that you was working for the other team. Had you not informed him who you were this conversation might've been different. I might've been the one in the hot seat." Smiling as Hoffman walked towards Gormez and stood beside him.

"Meet my good friend detective Hoffman."

- - - - -

Secretary of State, Agent Williams and many federal agents stood at the top of the mountain as they searched the surrounding area and found nothing indicating Johnson was there. Williams heard a horn sound off and began looking through his night vision binoculars and zoomed in on a tub boat that was several yards out to sea.

Williams adjusted the binoculars and noticed what appeared to be a man hanging from a hook on the tub boat. Then he zoomed in further and saw the sharks circling below in the water. He automatically knew it had to be Johnson and his old friend on the boat. He leaped into action and radioed for back up and support of the coast guards.

"Assistance needed federal agent down. Move in on her tub boat. Sixty yards point west." Federal agent need help Pronto he shouted over and over on the radio.

Air Force and Coast guards were on the tail of the boat in matter of minutes. Gormez noticed the air strike and screamed to the Captain,

" Lower that bastard to his death." As he took off walking with Carlos, Hoffman, Jimmy and Santana following him.

Captain began lowering the line when a sniper from the coast guard let off a shot hitting him in the neck, sending him over the side of the boat in the path of the sharks. Of course Captain was never found. Agents surrounded and invaded the boat. Gormez's foot soldiers, at least two dozen men, fired at the guards knocking them off the boat one by one. One of Gormez's men fired a rocket launcher, hitting one of the coast guard boats causing it to explode on impact. Men jumped from the boat to survival only to be attacked by the sharks.

Williams looking into the night vision informed the coast guards and federal agents to pull back as soon as he noticed that the agents were able to retrieve Agent Johnson. The agents had Johnson on a speed boat heading back to shore to meet with Williams. The federal agents and coast guards abandoned ship as ordered.

Once agent Johnson arrived back on shore, Williams ordered an air strike. Two F16 jets appeared out of nowhere and dropped two napalm bombs which exploded killing everybody on board.

Some of Gormez men jumped into the ocean off instincts forgetting what swam beneath the boat. Williams spotted another speed boat fleeing the scene but he wasn't sure if it was Gormrez. The case was then closed due to so many unidentifiable bodies found and not found, including some of his agents. Detective Hoffman's badge and ripped uniform with what appeared to be shark bites was found days later washed up on shore.

# CHAPTER 21

The following morning Joey called an emergency meeting with the NTP family at the stash house. The N.T.P. Family was growing stronger and bigger by the day. A.J. was now an official member. A.J. supplied the information about Jackie being the witness who snitched on them to officer Hoffman. He also told them about the Mark Wilson encounter in jail so NTP knew to look out for Mark's retaliation.

Joey let the crew know Paula's relation to Pedro Gormez.

"There we have it. We can link information to your girl Joey." Tyson continued to explain. "I believe she will pass the information to whoever his connect is. And if it's a family thing which with Mexican's we can bet that it is."

"What if it's not?" Dantwan scratched his head.

"Then we just have to let the police find Tony's body and soon the information will leak to whoever the dope belongs too."

Tyson had also paid the owner of the shooting gallery to use the house for a couple of days and not to go inside until he called with further details.

"Joey you good about leaking information to your girl?" Tyson wanted to make sure his homie wasn't too far gone.

"Man I think I love her but I love my niggas more." Joey smiled.

"Well, I think this meeting is over." Tyson tapped the table. "Oh Joey make sure to handle that snitch Jackie and off that nigga Larry as well. He knows too much."

"I don't think Reader will be down with move. That's her family dog." Dantwan chimed in looking at Joey.

"I'll worry about Reader, you just do your part, alright."

"Aight partner."

The men stood from the table and gave each other dap and hugs, representations their love and loyalty to the family. The men walked towards the door to feeling the nice breeze hit their faces as they parted ways.

- - - - -

Paula was sitting around the house waiting on Joey to call. She had been thinking about the way he made lover to her and smiled from ear to ear. paula got up from the couch to grab the remote control off the table to turn on the T.v. Then walked into their kitchen to get something to drink. After walking back into the living room her phone began ringing.

"Hello."

"Listen and listen carefully. The guy that killed those people in that house that burned down a few months back at the shooting gallery as we speak. If you want payback you better move on him now. I will not call you again." The man disconnected the call before Paula could ask any questions.

Paula stood there in shock that someone would call her house with such a message. Who was that and how did they get my number. She got up to peep out her blinds to see if anyone was outside watching her place. How did they now who I was and my relation to Pedro. She walked over to her couch and reached under her couch grabbing her 380 Gormez got her for her sweet sixteen birthday.

Paula immediately called her uncle's private line.

"Sunshine what's the occasion for this call, everything alright?"

"We need to talk and we need to talk now."

Gormez immediately reached to turn down the Mexican music playing in the background.

"What's wrong?"

"Just send a car for me immediately."

Gormez yelled at someone in the room with him, "Send a car to my niece now!"

As Paula disconnected the call she walked to her bedroom grabbing her all black track suit to throw on. She checked the window again then put on her sneakers. Twenty minutes later a jet black limo pulled in front of her town house and several bodyguards exited the vehicle. Two men posted at the vehicle while the other two walked to escort Paula to the vehicle.

Thirty minutes later they pulled up at the Greenville-Spartanburg Airport. Paula exited the limo following one of the bodyguards to a private jet. Two of the bodyguards holding submachine guns boarded the plan with her. The jet took off into the high blue skies.

One hour later they landed in Panama where the jet refueled and took off again and landed in Columbia an hour later. Paula was met by Gormez, Carlos, and Shantez. Gormez reached for Paula's hand and kissed her forehead.

"Uncle, We have to talk right now and I have to get back to the states as soon as possible."

They began walking away from the group as Paula began explaining the phone call she received. Gormez waved at Jimmy, Carlos and Shantez to come to him. Then he gave them the same information. The men knew exactly what had to be done. Carlos made a phone call to the states to have a hit team take position at the shooting gallery. The hit team was instructed not to move in until he arrived. Paula Carlos Jimmy and Shantez and the two bodyguards boarded the jet back to the states leaving Gormez watching as they took off.

- - - - -

Joey pulled up on Reader who was standing on the block making a sell to a fein.

"Yo Reader, jump in." Joey turned down the music bumping from his car speakers.

Reader ran over to the car and jumped in looking back at all the niggas watching on the corner wishing they were in her position.

"What's happening baby."

"We need to talk about your peeps, Jackie."

"Fuck that bitch Red. She ain't shit. Her and that fuck boy Larry stole my stash this morning." I just know it was then."

"You bullshitting!"

"I know it was them man."

Joey let Reader know that Jackie ratted them out to the police. He then proceeded to tell her the penalty for snitching and what they plan to do to Jackie and Larry.

"Check this out Joey baby, that's my sister though."

Joey cut her off and yelled, "That's yo who? The way she treated you at your worst."

"I know man but that's my sister. She took care of my daughter when I couldn't." Reader dropped her head feeling ashamed and hurt.

"You mean to tell me that lil Lorey is your daughter?"

Joey suddenly felt bad for evening considering Reader would be ok with marking her own sister.

"Yep."

"Damn this changes things."

Joey looked over at Reader as he rode up Rebecca Street in Nicole Town. He was thinking of how to handle Larry and Jackie without Reader being involved or her knowing that he was involved too even though she knew the NTP's family plan. Would she tell or stay real to the family?

Joey passed a small grey house on the left turning onto Ackley Road.

"You remember when I use to stay there Joey, before my mother and father passed away." Reader stared at the house she grew up in.

"Yeah, I remember everything babygirl."

Joey pulled the car over on Beachwood Avenue and parked on the side of the street and turned towards Reader.

"Check this out Reader, what are you doing tonight?"

"The same thing I do every night. Tryin' to put the block on smash."

They began laughing.

"Well take tomorrow night off. We are going to have diner with the family and then afterwards going to a party. Wear your best." He handed Reader ten thousand dollars as a bonus for all of her hard work.

Reader looked at Joey with watery eyes as a tear fell down her cheek. She wiped the tear away with her left hand and another fell from her right eye.

"Boy I love you til' death do us part. If it wasn't for you I might be dead already. Boy I would murk my own mother for you."

"Come on Reader don't start that emotional shit. We got business to handle."

Joey then took a deep breath to shake his emotions off because he felt his eyes tearing up as he looked at Reader who was as beautiful as her child hood days. She's all the way back. But Joey knew that starting a relationship with Reader would mess up their bond.

Joey started the car and took off making a u-turn on Beachwood Avenue heading up Ackley Road making a right turn and a quick left on Maco Street. Joey rode back to Fieldcrest Apartment and pulled on the block to drop Reader off.

Before getting out of the car Reader grabbed Joey's hand and squeezing it, "Remember always i belong to you."

As Joey pulled off he looked into the rear view mirror and watched Reader who stood in the center of the block yelling.

"Double Yokes for 15 dollars! Come get it while happy hour is popping! The fiends came running from every direction waving money.

# CHAPTER 22

Tyson returned home after the family meeting to find Tony dressed in a red negligé with matching red pumps, slowly sucking a red Charms blow pop.

"Hey honey, I've been waiting on you." She began walking towards Tyson swinging her hips seductively.

Tyson was about to respond, Tonya placed her index finger up to her lips signaling for him to be quiet. Tonya waled over to Tyson swinging her hips and grabbed his hand. She led him to their bedroom. She softly pushed him down on the bed and positioned to get on top of him.

Tyson grabbed her hips in an effort to slow down the heated passion the circled the room.

"We are going o dinner and a party tomorrow night, so dress to shine baby."

Tonya brought her mouth off Tyson's chest, "what's the occasion baby?" Removing the hair from her face.

Tyson couldn't tell her the truth just yet. He didn't want her to know that it was a party for Reader and A.J. being initiated into the family. To believe it or not Tonya didn't know about Tyson's organized crime family and his criminal activity.

"It's just a get together for the boys to celebrate Shammond

Williams being drafted into the NBA."

"You talking about Reggie Eps little brother." Tonya asked thinking back to when her ex-girlfriend used to date Reggie.

"Yeah that's him." Tyson replied lying again.

Tonya proceeded to kissing and licking Tyson's nipples then retreated off the bed.

"Where you going baby/"

"I'll be right back." Walking seductively, out of the room.

Tyson sat up on the bed leaning against the headboard waiting for Tonya to return when his phone started ringing.

"Yeah tell it." Tyson looked towards the door to see if Tonya was coming.

"The bug was planted and we watched her get picked up by a limo. We tailed her to the airport, she boarded a private jet."

"Good Dantwan, everything is going according to plan."

Tonya walked back into the room with two glasses of wine just as Tyson disconnected the line.

"Who you talking to baby?"

"Dee."

"What he want?" Handing him a glass of wine.

"Nothing, just wanted to know if we coming to the party tomorrow night." Tyson lied, placing the glass on the nightstand and grabbing Tonya by her waist.

Tonya leaned into Tyson to kiss him while he rubbed and squeezed her ass. He pulled her down on the bed to finish what she started.

- - - - -

Paula, Carlos, Jimmy and Shantez landed arrived in the states where a limo was already awaiting their arrival. Paula was taken back to her town house and informed that she can return to work at the Citgo immediately and to give her manager a call.

Then limo headed towards the shooting gallery where twenty Mexican men were waiting and staking out the gallery. Once Carlos, and Shantez got out the limo the Mexicans came out of their hiding places with weapons.

The limo drove off as dope fiends, dealers, and random people loitering the area began moving and running, thinking the Mexicans were part of a police raid. The owner of the house immediately called the police, which he was paid to do, letting them know someone had been murdered on his property.

Carlos and the men bum rushed into the gallery kicking in the front, side, and back doors. They began ram shacking the house, turning over tables and furniture. At the same time about twenty police cars, vans, and trucks pulled up on the scene. The police surrounded the premises.

"Come out with your hands up!" As several snipers moved in position.

Carlos ran to the window and saw they were surrounded by police not knowing that the owner was promised money and an ounce of heroin by Tyson to set this in motion.

"Mego, The police have us surrounded!"

"What are we going to do?" Shantez felt like a rat in a trap, hoping Carlos would advise them to surrender but a part of him knew Carlos was logo as fuck.

"There's a time to live and there's a time to die. Today seems like a good day to kill or die." Snatching the two 45 handguns from his holsters he ordered the ten men in the gallery to prepare to fire.

Carlos then placed his hand on his ear piece and began talking to Jimmy who was stationed a block away. Jimmy was already watching the scene from a distance and knew exactly what to do next.

Carlos fired the first shot causing an all out gun fight. Jimmy took off in the direction of the gallery with his men. They boxed the police in and began spraying their automatic weapons. Cops were dropping like flies as reinforcement appeared out of nowhere boxing in Jimmy and the crew. Mexicans hitting the grounds.

The crew inside the gallery fled outside blasting, leading the group was Carlos, who was the first to digest a bullet in the mouth and several in the chest. One after another bullets hit the Mexicans until three Mexicans remained and surrendered. Among the three men was Shantez.

Shantez was handcuffed and shoved into a police cruiser with the other two men and escorted to the Greenville County Jail where they were questioned but held their loyalty. An hour after being interrogated the men were picked up by five Federal agents and escorted to a secret location. Once at the secret location the men were separated. Shantez was talking to an officer when a familiar face greeted him.

"How are you doing Shantez Gomez?" Agent Johnson smirked as Shantez's eyes stared back cold as ice.

The gunfight was all over every news stations stating the mob killings of at least ten police offers and several Mexicans. One of the news reporters called it, 'The Mexican Massacre.'

The entire NTP family watched the broadcast at their different locations. Tyson then called a meeting. Joey called Reader to let her know that she needed to be at the meeting too. One hour later they met at the one bedroom house they kept their stash at.

Tyson opened the meeting letting them know this is their last meeting at this location.

"We have a new meeting spot, the *Safe Haven*."

The Safe Haven was three houses down from Tyson and Tonya's house. But he already told Tonya to find another house. They got a four bedroom, two baths, with a swimming pool, jacuzzi, and three car garage. The back yard ran off into a private golf course with a lake in the middle.

"Okay everybody let's ride to the new and improved Safe Haven and nobody can no about our new spot."

Tyson got up from his chair walking towards the door with his NTP family following him. Each hoped into their own cars trailing behind him. Twenty minutes later they pulled up to the new spot. Exited their vehicles and walked into the house.

Tyson led them to the conference room where a round marble table sat with eight chairs. Four large T.V. screens hung on the walls which doubled as monitors showing the surroundings of the house. The NTP family members took their seats as Tyson sat at the head of the table.

- - - - -

Paula and Mr. Gormez watched the new broadcast while talking over the phone. The news reporter began calling out a list of names of the men found murdered in the *Mexican Massacre,* also being called the O.K. Coral by some.

*"Tony Sloan, Carlos Gomez, Jimmy Sosa…"*

The reporter also mentioned that the authorities believed the hoot out was related to the death of Raymond Hall, Julio, Paps, and Mike Wilson. Mr. Gormez and Paula's mouth dropped to the floor at the mention of two kilo's of pure heroin being found on the scene along with several ounces of cocaine.

Before Tyson left the gallery previously he took the three ounces of heroin and stretched in with quinine. Knowing that the reporters would stretch the truth and Gormez would thinking that all the product was there and there was no way of getting it back. And as far as the money he would have to charge it to the game.

"Damn!" Gomez screamed into the receiver scaring Paula.

"What's wrong Papi?"

"I have to go away for a little while but you will be taken care of. Also Sara received your check today."

"What check?"

"A check for a million dollars from Pedro's insurance policy. I made you the beneficiary."

"What!"

"Listen Sunshine. There's also a checking account in your name with another million in it. You're going to the alright but I have to go." Gormez abruptly ended the call.

Paula heard the beep indicating the call had ended before she could ask her Papi any other questions. She sat on her bed turning the T.V. off staring into space panicking that she was loosing all of her family. She grabbed a pillow and stuffed her face into it crying herself to sleep.

# CHAPTER 23

Agent Johnson stood looking through a large mirror in a small room padded with soft cushion on the walls. A desk sat in the middle of the room and on the other side of the mirror agents watched him as he walked over to the table and slammed some files down. Staring at Shantez in the eyes,

"So tell me, where is Jesus Gormez?"

"I don't know nobody by that name agent." Returning a stare with a evil grin letting the words agent fall from his lips like maple syrup.

"So you want to play a tough guy huh?" Walking around the table closing in on Shantez who was still in handcuffs. "How does a natural life sentence without eligibility of parol sound to you?" Grabbing Shantez by the chin with his face so close that Shantez could feel the hot heat from his breath.

"Life sentence for what?" Shantez knew agent Johnson didn't have anything on him.

"For the murders of ten police officers and the twenty plus Mexican Massacre."

"Prove it." Shantez smiled at Johnson just as two other agents walked into the room. The agents had telephone books under their arms.

"Ok, I tried to give you a fair shake and you spit in my face. So now you'll have to deal with the muscle." Johnson walked over to the surveillance mirror and pulled the black curtain closed.

The two agents walked over to Shantez and began removing his shoes.

"What are y'all doing? Shantez eyes got as big as flying saucers.

"The same thing y'all do, get down for ours." Johnson laughed at the fear in Shantez's eyes as one of the agents placed a phone book to the side of Shantez's face.

"Last chance." Johnson smiled ear to ear.

"Fuck you pig."

Followed by a blow to the head. The agent punched the side of the phone book to prevent scars from appearing. The other agent grabbed Shantez's foot and began beating it with a flash light causing damage to the arch in his right foot. After ten minutes of police brutality Johnson stopped the agents,

"Do you want to talk now or do we have to continue this process? As you know here in South Carolina the hands of one is the hands of all and I'm sure we can find your finger prints on one of the guns we collected at the crime scene."

Shantez cleared his throat as he began sweating.

"Look punk! I'm trying to help you!" We know all about the pretty little girls you have in Texas and your little boy in Mexico. I'm mored than sure that you would like to see them again. Now if you don't want to cooperate with us, I'm sure one of your comrades down the hall will. Besides I'd hate to have to let the muscle bust your ass. You can file whatever las suit you want to while you serving a life sentence. The ball is in your court. And remember we are the United States Federal Government, there is no win with us. Do you understand?

"Where is my lawyer. I am entitled to representation. So before I say anything to any of you pigs, I please the fifth." Shantez smirked.

Johnson paced the room thinking about how cocky Shantez was and knew he had to take a different approach.

"Good try but here is a better one. Since you want to play hard ball let me pitch you a curve ball. We both know that you are an illegal immigrant with no green card, so you don't have a right to shit! I will personally make sure you serve your time here for violating our national laws. And on top of that green card, I'll make certain your paperwork gets lost in the system and by the time it resurfaces it will be twenty years later.  Now do you see how serious this shit is or you too stupid to help your self?

Shantez looked at Agent Johnson and realized that there was no way out of his situation. By the looks of it his only options were to turn coat and snitch on his step father Jesus Gormez.

"Look Shantez we do not want you but we will take you down if we can't get Jesus Gomez with you help. So here is the final offer, so take it or leave it. You will receive immunity from prosecution of any and all charges concerning the police and Mexican murders. I will also provide you with a new identity and move your family into witness protection program. Live a low profile and simple life as a free man. How does that sound? And in return all we want is Jesus's location, phone numbers, cars he drives, how many kids he has, how many murders he's committed and ordered, and how many hairs he has around his asshole. We want everything on him. We will catch him, you can believe that!

Shantez stared at Johnson. He knew if he testified against Gomez he was as good as dead. But if he didn't he face time in jail and may never see his kids again.

"If you choose to accept this deal then back out later, I will prosecute you to the fullest extent of the law. And I'll make sure the entire underground will know that you're a snitch. Now do you understand?

"What do you want to know?"

- - - - -

Several hours later the NTP family met at the Safe Haven after each member completed their task concerning the robbery and murder of Pedro Gomez. Sitting at the round table Tyson opened the discussion with,

"Okay everybody listen up. Joey what's the first topic of discussion?" Eyeing the two new members of the family to make sure he had their attention.

"Well everything has been going according to plan except we got a few loose end that need to be tied up."

"Like what?" Not liking the sound of that.

"The Jackie and Larry incident still hanging in the air." Joey glanced at Reader to see her reaction.

"What that bitch done did now?" Reader asked getting tired of Jackie's bullshit.

"Same thing baby girl." Joey leveled a stern look at Reader as he felt she was out of place being a new comer.

The family discussed how Jackie was the one who snitched on Joey and AJ murdering Mike Wilson. Reader listened without showing any emotion. She also knew how snitch niggas or bitches get dealt with and now that she's a member of the NTP crew, that was her new family.

"So how do you want to handle it Joey?" Tyson looked at Reader for her reaction then looked at Joey.

"Don't worry. I'll handle Jackie since that's my sister." Dropping her head down.

"You do understand what we're asking you to do right, Reader?"

"Yeah. Do I look stupid or something?" She snapped at Tyson.

"You my girl Reader but are you sure you can handle this, I'll do it for you." Dantwan put his hand on Readers shoulder for comfort.

"I got this." Reader lifted her head with a wicked smile on her face. "Consider the problem solved."

"Aight. Anything else on the plate for today's discussion?" Tyson asked around the table.

"What about Mike's little brother, Mark?" A.J. asked.

"Don't worry about him. I think I got a couple of cats in county that can handle that. What y'all think?"

"We might be able to use him in the long run but it really depends on how this entire thing plays out." Joey thought it would be a good idea to hold off on taking Mark out.

"Well we'll hold off on his ass then but if I hear anything about him trying to revenge his brothers death we'll do him quick."

"What's wrong with Dantwan? You look sick boy." Reader asked.

"That nigga thinking about that girl." A.J. laughed.

"Who?" Joey confused.

"Crazy ass Lisa." A.J. blurted out as the crew began laughing.

"She finally got your ass." Tyson laughed.

"It ain't even like that dog."

"It's all good. Everybody need someone inhere life and Lisa might just be the one for you. She might even slow your crazy ass down. Just don't let her distract you from your duties to the family. Don't want to have to deal with her too."

Tyson laughed at that last statement but Dantwan knew he was serious as a heart attack about taking Lisa out if he felt she threatened the livelihood of the NTP family.

"Once last thing to address then I'll let y'all go. I'm expecting all of y'all at the party tomorrow night. And as usual dress to kill. You can bring a plus one or come solo it doesn't matter. Everybody that's somebody will be attending and I want my crew stunting like never before. Even thought we're there to have fun, keep your eyes open and ears listening."

Everybody agreed and the meeting was closed. The family got up from the round table and hugged one another as they exited the Safe Haven to their cars.

"Joey?"

"Yeah what's up?" Walking backwards towards Tyson.

"You think Reader can handle that?"

"I don't know but if she can't I will." Joey watched Reader get into the car.

"You do know that if she fails, you gone have to take her out too."

"I know and I'm sure she knows it too. So I believe she will handle her end."

Joey was hoping that he was right about Reader. That's his homie and he didn't want to have to kill her too. But he knew if she failed he'd have to lose his friend.

"Okay I'll see you at the party." Tyson walked to the back of the house as Joey walked to the car.

"You readers to roll?" He looked over at Reader in the passenger seat.

"Let's go." Reader replied as they drove off down the street making a right and quick left turn.

# CHAPTER 24

Joey and Reader rode down Laurens Road coming off the motor mile out of Mauldin they passed Gower Park.

"You straight with this? You know what to do right?" Glancing at Reader as he passed the Great Escape bike shop.

"Yeah nigga. why you keep asking me the same question, like I'm dumb or something?"

"Ok boo damn, calm down. I was just making sure we all come out of this safe and sound." Joey slowed the car down making a left run on Ackley Road.

They rode in silence for the next five minutes going through the back streets of Nicole Town Community before Joey decided to call Paula as he turned down Rebecca street.

"Hello." Paula answered in a sleepy voice.

"What's happening baby girl?"

"You." Paula replied sitting up on the couch she was napping on.

"What you doing?" Joey smiled thinking about the sex they had the other night.

"I was sleep, waiting on you to call. When you coming through?"

"Give me a couple of hours. I have to handle some business

right now."

"Ok, I'll see you when you get here."

They made kissing sounds over the phone as they disconnected their cal. Reader started laughing as she eased dropped.

"Nigga you sprung."

"Well, you need to get you some and you'll get sprung too."

"I will in just a matter of time." Reader looked at Joey with lust in her eyes as she licked her lips.

Joey damn near rammed a car from the back as Reader touch his leg.

"Watch what the hell you doing boy!" Reader shouted.

"My bad."

Reader Tucker was not an ugly broad by far but it was just her pass life chasing crack pipe, which caused Joey and others to assume that she turned tricks for drugs but she never did. Reader was a hustler. She hustled for every dime and high that she had. If she wanted to have sex, she did it because she wanted to not because she wanted drugs. She had a male sex partner who was a casual smoker.

Since Reader stopped smoking she gained all of her weight back. Weighing one hundred and sixty pounds, thick in the ass and slim in the waist. Such a pretty girl with a razor scar about four inches above her right ear. She got that scar from Jackie a few years back before she started smoking crack. They got into a fight because Jackie had sex with Reader's boyfriend Willie. Willie said that Jackie was jail bait after getting her pregnant and continued his relationship with Reader. A few months later ended up getting her pregnant too. Once Reader was pregnant Willie introduced her to crack cocaine and turned her out and that was the beginning of her downfall.

Joey pulled off Rebecca Street, making a left and turning on to Elder Street. He oiled down by a wooded area with a path that lead to Fieldcrest apartments. Joey parked the car and looked over at Reader.

"Yo, I'm going to park right here and wait on you. You ready to get down for yours?"

"Huh?" Reader rubbed the scar above her ear.

"I said, are you ready to get down for the family?"

"Yeah let's roll."

Reader began opening the passenger side door. Joey popped the truck as he got out of the car. He walked around to the trunk. Reader grabbed a 380 handgun filled with cop killers and tucked it into her waist band. She then grabbed one of the plastic ski mask and a pair of surgeon gloves and put them on. She then removed the gun and wiped it clean to remove her finger prints. Joey then handed Reader a big black rain coat with a hood and she slipped it over her body.

"I'll be close behind and make me a proud father." Laughing at his own statement but Reader didn't see the humor in it but she still laughed before disappearing into the woods entering Fieldcrest.

Sitting ten yards away from Jackie's back door she sat and watched for five minutes. She then saw her daughter Lorey and her two cousins, Eric and Brian.

"Oh shit! I forgot about them. Fuck it! I gotta do what I gotta do.

Reader slipped on the mask, pulling the 380 from her waist and screwed on the silencer. She then pulled the hood over her head. The children ran around the apartment chasing each other.

Reader took off running like a track star towards Jackie's back door when the children ran towards the front of the apartment. Her high school track skills came in handy as she quickly got to the back door which was open. She pulled the screen door and slid into the kitchen without being seen. She heard voices upstairs so she slid through the apartment without making a sound, crawling the staircase. Once at the top of the staircase she was able to hear Jackie and Larry talking in her bedroom.

"Fuck that nigga, he shitted on me."

"Damn girl! Why you on that nigga dick like that?"

"Well, he wont be around too much longer, his ass going to jail for killing Mike."

"What the fuck you talking about Jackie?"

"You'll see."

"Girl you crazy. What'cho done did now?"

"Police asked me and I told them what I saw." Jackie lied knowing she went to the police station on her own and offered information on the murder.

"Say what?"

"You heard me nigga."

"Bitch you crazy!"

Reader hearing the entire conversation knew that Larry didn't have anything to do with it but she had an order from NTP to fulfill.

"You should have robbed that nigga when I told you too."

Reader continued to listen clutching her 380 then kicked the bed room door in and let off two shots, ripping threw Larry's chest exploding on contact. Jackie stood there frozen.

"Please don't kill me."

Reader removed her mask and hood and looked at Jackie. Jackie was relieved to see that it was her big sister and took a deep breath. Jackie recalled that Larry stole a package of crack from Reader earlier that day and reached on the dresser to retrieve it. She reached her hand out to Reader as she noticed a tear drop rolling down her big sister's face. Reader don't, were Jackie's last words as a bullet ripped through her head leaving brain fragments all over her the wall.

Jackie's body slid down next to the bed as Reader pulled out two ounces of dope and placed it in Larry's pocket. Then began dropping more crack around the room and down the stairs staging the scene.

Reader stepped out the back door of the apartment and her daughter, Lorey was standing there with the prettiest little doll face one would ever see.

"Moma." Lorey opened her arms in the air reaching for Reader.

Reader stared at her daughter and began placing on her hood and mask. Lorey tried to grab her leg but she moved her out the way and took off running. Lorey watched her mother disappear into the wooded area.

Five minutes later she meet back up with Joey. When she got there Joey was leaning on the car hood. Joey saw the tears forming in Reader's eyes as she fell into his opened arms and cried like a baby.

"It's going to be ok babygirl. I got you." Joey kissed her softly on the side of her neck.

They got back into the car and she explained everything including the children being there. Joey immediately made a call to Tyson who told them to head back to get the children. Tyson had a weak spot for children and would never abandon them. Joey and Reader took the long way back to the apartment.

The two little boys that was at the apartment found Jackie and Larry dead in the bedroom and went to the neighbors apartment for help. The police arrived twenty minutes later. Joey and Reader arrived shortly after and jumped into character.

"What happened?" Joey asked walking toward the front of the apartment, going under the yellow tape that roped off the scene.

"Hold up son." One of the officers attempted to block Joey's entrance.

Reader walked over to Joey and the officer letting the officer know this was her sisters apartment and she was coming to pick up the children. The officer stepped aside to allow them entrance.

Reader's daughter and the two boys, Brian and Eric, were sitting in the back seat of a police car crying. The officer informed Reader that Lorey had been crying and pointing towards the woods for her mother.

"I'll take the children home with me now."

"Well please leave a name and number in case we have any questions."

"No problem sir." Writing down her cell number and old address.

"Thank you ma'am."

Reader removed the children from the police car and led them to Joeys car.

"Put your seatbelts on."

Joey drove Reader and the children to her new two bedroom condo in Taylors.

"I'll pick you up for the party tomorrow night so find a baby sitter."

Reader threw up her middle finger as Joey laughed and drove off.

# CHAPTER 25

After agent Johnson finished questioning Shantez, he issued a warranty for Tony Sloan to search his mother's house. During the search they found guns there were used to kill Mike Wilson, Raymond Hill, Pedro Gormez, Julio and Papi.

Johnson knew something was off. There's no way Tony did all of this by himself, especially robbing Gormez's stash house. He felt that Shantez had to be lying to him.

Johnson further concluded that even if Tony's partner in crime, Hound, lent a helping hand in the robberies and deaths things still wasn't adding up. But also knew that if Gormez had anything to do with Hounds disappearance he'd never be found due to Gormez's clean up crew that he is now aware of thanks to Shantez.

Shantez was placed into witness protection and given a new identity. He would not surface again until they caught Jesus and put him behind bars for life. However, it was too late for his family. They were found butchered by the time the Federal agents got to them.

Johnson's gut was telling him that things were not adding up. His initial witness, Jackie, gave Joey as the killer of Mike Wilson and now she's dead.

Johnson felt there were too many unanswered questions. And

with Johnson's eagerness to bring down Jesus Gormez he wouldn't close the case just yet. Instead he put out an ABP on Joey so that he could be brought in for questioning for the murder of Mike Wilson.

- - - - -

"Mark Wilson." One of the prison guards shouted into the bullpen.

"Yeah. What's up?"

"Pack your things you're out."

Mark ran fast as he could back to his cell giving dap and pounds along the way to the other inmates as he went to gather his belongings.

"Don't you come back now." Advised from an old black man up for doing his fourth sentence if he didn't beat the first degree murder that hung over his head.

"Yeah old timer."

After Mark got his things he walked to the gate to be escorted down stairs to collect his street clothes and to be checked out. His clothes wreaked of mildew so he trashed them as he walked over to the pay phones to call his partner to come pick him up.

After waiting twenty minutes in the parking lot a blue crown Vic dripping in candy paint laced in chrome and sitting on twenty six inches pulled in front of him.

"Come on nigga." The driver shouted.

Mark looked to see who it was.

"What's up my nigga." Mark excited to see his boy Chop in the flesh.

"Aint shit just trying to get this paper." Chop smiles as Mark settled into the baby blue seat of the car.

"Boy how long you been in county?"

"Shit they had me locked down for two years then they brought me back to county for eighteen months. I went to court last week and the judge gave me time served for the assault and battery with attempt to kill."

"Boy I heard about your brother man. I told him about fucking with that bitch nigga Tony. You know he got smoked last nigh too."

"Yeah I been hearing all types of stories. I don't know what to think."

Marked watched the area as Chop turned on Laurens road heading towards Greenline Community. Chop pulled out a blunt and lit it taking two buffs before passing it to Mark.

"That's what I'm talking about." Mark inhaled smoke into his lungs.

"So what you going to do about the nigga that killed your brother?"

"You act like you know something. Tell me what' s poppin' homie."

"Word on the street was that Tony did it, even the police think Tony did it but the O.G's on the street saying it was this cat name Dantwan. Word is he stood over Mike and dumped a whole clip in him. They saying the shit was over some girl name Lisa."

"A bitch! Come on man. Nigga's don't kill over bitches."

"Well that's the word on the streets."

"Who the hell is Dantwan?"

Chop pulled into a parking lot into some new Townhouses in

Greenline. "You know that nigga that be with A.J." Pulling a bag from under his seat.

"Yeah, I remember him. Yeah, I'mma have to pay that nigga a little visit real soon."

"Boy I hope you know what you doing. Since you been locked up them boys got heavy in the game. I'm talkin' Mexican mafia type shit. Nigga you been watching the news? Them niggas feeding the blocks now."

"Mexican mafia or not, somebody gone pay for my brothers death. And I'm looking for the trigger man."

"Well tonight you'll get your chance because them cats thrown a big part at the club off airport road. All the ballers and players gone be there and I'm be right up in that bitch too."

"Well soon as I get straight I'm trying to be up in that bitch too. But first I need some fresh gear and to holla at a couple of homies for some grands."

"Nigga don't worry I got you but that other shit about revenging your brother's death, I'm not with that shit. No offense , Mike was cool and everything and you're my man but I'm tryin' but I'm tryin' to get this money and take care of my kids and a nigga can't do none of that from prison or dead."

"I feel ya man. I'll handle that on my own."

Chop pulled into his parking space in front of his townhouse.

"Come on let's get something to eat and you out them jail house rags then we can go get some pussy."

Chop and Mark ate and smoked another blunt while they swallowed couple shots of Tequila. Chop took Mark to his home girls house and paid her two hundred to show Mark a good time.

# CHAPTER 26

Club Enterprise was packed wall to wall. The line to get in was a mile long with people of all walks of life from groupies to wanna be ballers. A few thugs and hustlers stood in the parking lot twisting blunts, blasting music, and getting blazed before going inside. They cackled at the women that passed by and sometimes grabbed a handful of ass.

Amongst the young thugs gathering at their cars representing their districts were, District 25, City Heights, Fieldcrest, Green Avenue, Piedmont Manor, Cannaberry, Lakeshore, Woodland Holmes, West Greenville, Sterling, and Nicholtown. The whole Greenville came out to have a good time. As you looked out into the parking lot with each hood segregated into sections bumping their music you knew everybody came to have get to fucked up and have a good time.

A big boy black Bentley pulled up to the entrance of the club sitting on Gotti wheel rims. The Bentley was draped in gold chrome with a kit to match. The driver, Big Willie, exited the vehicle looking like Suge Knight from the Death Row record label. Big Willie not only pushed his share of heroin and cocaine in Greenville, he pushed it outside of Greenville City limits to Spartanburg, Greenwood, and Newberry. Big Willie had on an all black leather three piece suit with black gators. He had a ring on his pinky finger the size of a nickel and that was all he needed to complete his look. He skipped the long line and made his way to the red carpet as the valet parked his car in VIP parking with security.

Next to pull up to the front entrance was a money green Benz with gold glitter specs with gold tinted windows trimmed in gold. Everybody eyes was glued on the vehicle waiting to see who was going to step out. As the Alligator rims came to a stop you could see the license plate that read NTP and the front tag read Fuck the World Records. There was so many oohs and ahh's from the crowd and the NTP family knew there would be.

Dyson stepped out of the car with an all leather Pelle Pelle jumpsuit and a Cuban link with a medallion flooded with diamonds hanging from his neck. The medallion was engraved with NTP on it. He also had a matching Movado watch across his wrist and pinky ring that totaled no less than fifteen grand.

"Yo Dyson, what's happening boy?" A young cat from Nicholtown yelled out through the crowd standing amongst the Nicholtown crew.

"Pressure, baby pressure." Dyson replied as he continued moving across the red carpet into the club.

Then you could hear another car coming as music from the speakers blasted. A candy apple red coupdaville sitting on twenty-six inch rims draped in chrome with T.V's in the headrest pulled up.The driver jumped out the car smiling ear to ear with another cat following behind. The second cat stood 6ft.2 and weighed 240 pounds solid. The two men walked towards the entrance as their car was parked in VIP parking. The driver was known through Greenville by the name, Mayor but known to the Nichol town community where he's from as Joel Williams. He's the reason a lot of cats from different hoods were able to feed their families. Joel had on a red and white South Pole riot gear with a iced out platinum chain with a Jesus piece flooded with blue gems. He also had on a multi colored Rolex that told time in four different countries. The big guy with Joey was Valentino who was also from Nichol town and hustled the block as Joey's henchman. Valentino over the years put in a lot of work for the neighborhood and was well respected for his body counts and loyalty.

After Mayor's car was turned off, the crowd still heard loud bass heading their way but had assumed it was Mayor's car until the sound got louder as the car came closer. A twin Cadillac Escalade sitting on Zebra rims made by Ashanti pulled up. Dantwan hopped out of the truck with his iced out platinum chain and medallion with NTP engraved in it the same as Dyson's necklace. Dantwan sported a patent leather Mecca sweatsuit with a pair of white on white forces on his feet and an international watch on his wrist. As he stepped out of his ride a bunch young thugs standing in the parking lot barked his name in excitement giving him his props. Dantwan walked over to the passenger side of his car and opened the door for his date. Lisa stepped out rocking an Apple Bottom jeans that snugged her ass perfectly with a matching jacket. Karen stepped out of the back seat wearing Perry Ellis from head to toe looking like she wasn't even old enough to get in the club.

Dantwan popped the truck to help Karen with A.J.'s wheel hair and help him out of the car. The young cat's from Nicholtown screamed out again calling A.J.'s name excited that he made it out of surgery alive from the gunshot wounds. A.J. Was wearing a red, black, yellow, and blue South Pole leather sweatsuit with the same NTP families crescent medallion.

As Dantwan, Karen, Lisa and A.J. made their way to the red carpet an identical truck pulled up but this one was cream. Tyson got out the truck wearing an all white Sean John dress suit with a matching brim with cream colored snake skin shoes. The same medallion necklace with NTP engraved on it hung around his neck. He had on a pinky ring the size of a dime and it shined like the fluorescent lights. Tyson walked to the passenger side of the truck and opened the door. He then reached in and grabbed Tony'a hand pulling her gently out of the truck. She had on a cream colored Sean John dress with a pair of white pumps and a string of white pearls around her neck. She wrapped up in Tyson's arms as they stood beside Dantwan and the others.

Joey then stepped out of the back of the truck wearing an all black Sean John suit with black gators. He sported the same medallion with NTP engraved but he had a pinky ring to match engraved with NTP in diamonds. Joey stepped to the side and allowed Paula to exit the truck. Her and Reader were in the truck watching a recording of the soap opera's.

"Come on ladies. Cut that T.V. off." Joey reached his hand inside the truck to grab Paula's hand.

Paula stepped out of the truck wearing an all black Perry Ellis dress with matching Perry Ellis heels. The dress stuck to her body like glue showing all of her curves. The young thugs around the blue mouths dropped at the sight of beauty and curves. Paula smiled and waved at everybody like she was Princess Dianna or somebody royal. Joey, Tyson, and Tonya began laughing but Paula didn't have the slightest idea what they were laughing at.

After Paula stood to the side with the rest of the NTP family, Joey reached for Readers hand. She hesitated to get out, she was nervous about her debut. Reader grabbed Joeys hand, wondering how the people would like her now being that she was not a crack head and was all the way back, curves and all. Joey pulled Reader from the car and everybody and their moma locked eyes on Reader amazed at her come back. Reader stepped closer to the NTP family looking as if she had just stepped off the show case. Thugs and ballers ooh'ed and ah'd and even cat called at her. The family laughed. Reader had on a fitted black dress. She had her hair let down with bouncy curls. Her and Paula were damn near dressed alike to a T except Reader wore the NTP medallion around her neck. The only other thing that was different was the color of their skin.

During the ride to the club Joey couldn't keep his eyes off Reader. She was beautiful and she loved every second that Joey stared at her. Tyson even glanced at Reader a couple of times until Tonya slapped him across the back of his head letting him know that he better keep his eyes on the road.

Paula on the other hand played green and really didn't care because Joey was giving her enough attention which also made Reader a little upset. As she only got dolled up for him and she wanted some of his attention as well.

The NTP family walked into the club and was immediately escorted to the VIP section where Tyson informative do the help to bring some drinks to the table.

"Sir y'all are the guest of honor there are several bottles of Moët already at the table." The cute waitress smiled at Tyson until she saw Tonya's mean mug and walked away.

The music was loud and the D.J. Was playing Eric B and Rakim paid in full.

"That's my song right there. Come on y'all let's dance." Lisa grabbed Dantwan by the arm.

Karen then jumped up form the table and grabbed A.J. pushing him to the floor to make sure her man had a good time too.

"No girl." A.J. embarrassed to be on the dance floor in a wheelchair.

"Shut up." Karen continued pushing him to the dance floor while the family laughed and D and Lisa followed behind.

"Joey excuse me for a second, I have to go to the ladies room." Paula stood up and kissed Joey on the cheek and went to the bathroom.

"Don't be long I might miss you boo." Joey said causing Paula to blush.

"Sprung, sprung, sprung." Reader said loud enough for Joey to hear giving him a look.

Joey flashed back to when Reader and him was in the car together when he almost crashed when she touched his leg and the look she gave him then is the same look she was giving him now.

"I'll be right back." Reader stood up preparing to walk off.

"Where you going?" Joey's words fall on death ears because Reader kept walking towards the crowd.

Tyson leaned over and whispered into Joey's ear,

"Boy you better be careful before you be sprung, sprung, sprung by two women." Laughing as Tonya grabbed his hand and lead him to the dance floor.

Tonya was set on having a good time because she had not been out partying since God knows how long. Reader returned with a drink in her. She needed something stronger than Moët. She sat down beside Joey and they watched the people in the club having a good time.

"You alright reader?"

Reader sucked her teeth giving Joey the silent treatment and said, " You stupid." Then got up and walked off again. This time she headed to the bathroom.

Joey made a mental note to find out what that was all about later. He needed to know what was going on in Readers' head but little did he know it was not the head he should be checking it was her heart.

# CHAPTER 27

Outside of club Enterprise a blue Crown Vic draped with chrome sitting on twenty-six inch rims pulled up to the entrance blasting Big Daddy Kane's Raw. Chop and Mark got out the car as the valet rushed to grab the keys to park the car. Chop and Mark was stunting as hard as they could but they were no match to the ballers and hustlers whole was already inside the club. Chop was wearing Tommy from head to toe with an iced out gold Cuban link with a Jesus piece laced in diamonds. He also rocked a Rolex with a matching bracelet. Mark was wearing Chop's Sean John sweatsuit, that played out last year. But he got by because it was fresh out the cleaner and still looked brand new. He also had on Chop's fake gold rope which Chop barely wore anymore.

They entered the club and the only reason that Mark was allowed into entered was because he was with Chop. Chop had a little bit of pull with the bouncer at the door because Chop always hit the bouncer off with cash money at other clubs when he went out.

"It's live up in this bitch." Chop stated looking around at the two girls dancing with each other while they was surrounded by half nude women.

"Yeah." Mark replied looking around still feeling like he was in jail.

"Calm down nigga, you aint locked up no more." Chop stated noticing Marks reaction to the girl that slightly bumped him as she passed by.

"Once I get a drink in me, I'll be just right." Mark replied looking at a baller wearing a platinum rope flooded with rubies and diamond dancing with there dime pieces.

"We'll lets hit the bar first." Walking towards the bar with Mark following him.

Chop and Mark made their way through the crowded club and stood at the bar.

"Let us get two hens on ice." Chop ordered, placing a fifty dollar bill on the bar.

The bartender left to fix the drinks as Chop and Mike stood there admiring the ballers, hustlers and players, knowing that one day they would have their chance at the pot of gold. Chop then turned towards Mark,

"Hey, that's that nigga right there." Looking out on the dance floor.

"Who?"

"That nigga Dantwan, right there doing the two step on the flo.' The one with the patent leather Mecca sweat suited air force one's on.

Mark began studying Dantwan's face so that he could remember him when it came time to seek revenge for his brothers death. As Mark studied Dantwan, Chop was getting their drinks from the bartender when a voice chimed behind him.

"Yo what up nigga?" Chop turned around to see who it was in

his hear.

"What's happening Mayor, my nigga!"

Chop had been getting drugs on assignment from the Mayor. Chop had also owed Joel a lot of money and had been ducking him. chap had no idea that Joel would be at the club because normally the Mayor didn't attend clubs and stuck strictly to his grin on the blocks.

"I been trying to get at you with those five grands." Chop lied.

"Where is my mothafucking money, nigga?" The Mayor shouted as Valentino stood beside him circling Chop and Mark.

"I got you man. I'm going to holla at you tomorrow."

"You think this is a mothafucking game nigga." The Mayor stared Chop down.

"Nah man, it aint like that, I got you word." Chop pleaded sounding like a little bitch as Mark watched and couldn't believe that Chop was letting Mayor talk to him like that.

Out of nowhere Mayor slapped the shit out of Chop, causing blood to drip from Chop's nose and mouth. The sound of the slap was loud enough to be heard by people near the bar and heads turned.

"Nigga, have my money tomorrow." Pointing his finger in Chop's face who was ducking his head every time the Mayor would talk and move his hand.

People stared until they realized that it was only the Mayor handling his business as usual so they returned to partying like it was 1999. The Mayor and Valentino then walked off and Mark looked at Chop,

"Damn nigga you let that nigga handle you like that. Especially in front of all these bitches?" Feeling like his man done lost major stripes and points in the game.

"It's cool man." Chop replied wiping the blood from his nose and mouth.

"Oh hell nah, you got to go serve that nigga now or I'm going to have to serve you nigga." Mark shouted bringing attention back on them.

"Chill nigga, them nigga's is major cats. I aint got money to go to war right now."

"I don't give a fuck how major them nigga's are. You need to go handle your business and you to handle it now." Mark got mad and didn't understand what Chop meant because he was renegade. All Mark could see is that Chop was acting like a bitch made nigga.

Mark then looked across the club and saw the Mayor smiling like nothing had happened. He noticed Mayor giving daps and his to a bunch of guys standing in the crowd near him, including Dantwan. He saw Mayor tilt his head towards the NTP medallion around Dantwan's neck as if he was a king

*"I'm going to rob, beat, and then kill them niggas."* Mark's scowled crossed the room at the crew.

Chop was embarrassed about being slapped and punched in the club so he let Mark know that he was ready to go. Mark agreed because he was embarrassed too that his homie got bitch slapped and didn't do nothing about it.

As Chop and Mark began walking towards the entrance to leave Mark detoured to the restroom.

"Hurry up man. I want to get out of here before some shit jump off."

Mark shook his head as he walked in to the restroom. *This punk motherfucker done let a nigga bitch slap him and now he's running like a bitch.*

As Mark was walking into the restroom, Paula was coming out of the ladies restroom and they bumped shoulders. Mark was already mad so he yelled out,

"Bitch! Watch where you going."

"Watch where the fuck you going fagot."

Mar then raised his hand to smackPaula but his hand was caught in mid air by Chop.

"Come on man, leave that drunk bitch alone."

"Ya moma's a drunk bitch, bitch. Looking at them eye to eye ready to kick, bite, and scratch.

Chop then let go of Marks hand so that he could do what he wanted to do to Paula. Reader then stepped out of nowhere.

"Yo little homie, you don't wanna go there."

Mark turned around and stared at Reader. They both sensed their faces looked familiar to each other but couldn't put a finger on it. Reader stood next to Paula as they faced off with Mark and Chop. Reader wasn't scared because she had her baby 380 pointed directly at them through her small purse.

"Let me get the fuck up out this spot, for I mark one of these punk as bitches or niggas." Mark stared at Reader and Paula with cold eyes.

"If anybody is going to get marked, it's going to be you bitch ass nigga. Now bring it." Reader stared at Mark waiting for him to make his move.

Mark began walking towards Reader and Paula with anger in his heart. Reader pulled the 380 out of her purse and stuck it in his face tapping his nose.

"So that's what you want to do nigga?" As oooh's and ahh's came from the small crowd that had gathered watching.

The crowd started moving back and Tyson noticed the commotion as he seen Reader in the midst of it. Tyson rushed off the dance floor leaving Tonya behind. He made his appearance known to Reader,

"Yo what's poppin' Reader?"

"This bitch as nigga here trying to get murked up in this bitch."

By the time Tyson looked back to address Mark, he'd walked off.

"Shit fuck em they gone now. Don't worry about them fuck nigga's."

"We wasn't." Paula quickly replied causing Tyson to smile. He liked the fact that she could handle her own if need be.

Just as they were walking back towards the dance floor the rest of the NTP family was approaching the area. The women had switch blades in hand while the men had guns in theirs.

"What up?" Dantwan yelled out hyped and ready to get to bangin'."

"Aint nothing Billy the Kid. Y'all go back to having a good time. Tyson waved them off as everybody laughed. Tyson joined Tonya as she watched Chop and Mark exit the club.

"I'm tired of dancing, let's go sit for a few in our VIP."

# CHAPTER 28

Back in the VIP section the NTP family continued to have a ball, popping bottles of Moët and Don P. They even shared the love by sending a few bottles of  Don P and Moët to other hustler's tables. As the family partied, Joey stood up and informed the family that him and Tyson had to go handle some business and they would be back in a few minutes. Tyson and Joey left the VIP and walked to another table in the club. Reader, Paula and Tonya watched Joey and Tyson sat at a table with big fat Willie. Tonya saw the snarl on reader's face as she looked over at the table. She didn't ask any questions because she didn't feel like it was her place to. But Reader continued to watch the fellas as the walked off into a small office on the other end of the club.

The rest of the family decided to continue their night of fun. Karen grabbed A.J."s wheelchair handle bars, "Round two, nigga." Pushing A.J. to the dance floor.

"No I'm tired baby." A.J. protested which was to no avail.

"How you gonna be tired and you sitting down nigga, shut up." Karen pushed him through the crowd as the rest of the family laughed.

Lisa and Dantwan then followed behind Karen to the dance floor while Paula and Reader sat at the table chatting it up, getting to know one another and ultimately becoming the best of friends. Other men in the club tried hitting on them but was cut short before they could get a, 'What's happening' out of their mouths. Tonya sat in the corner getting drunk laughing at everything.

"Paula?"

"Yes."

"Let's get fucked up."

"Girl is you crazy. You know Joey and them would cut a fool if they had to drag our asses out of here drunk."

"Shid, I don't know about y'all but I'm already feeling right and I'm going to get tighter."

Tonya chimed in laughing and talking sluggish with a glass of Hypnotic Hulk mixed with Hennessy in her hand, "What the hell, why not."

The ladies sat in VIP downing drink after drink until they were intoxicated and horny. Tonya stood up fro the table and almost fell but caught herself as all of them laughed. Tonya grabbed her glass and slurred her words, "Sisters I have to go for a minute but I'll be back in a minute. I see some old classmates by the bar." She walked off staggering.

"Alright girl, watch your step." Reader informed Tonya as all of them laughed and Tonya disappeared into the crowd.

Reader turned her attention onto Paula starring at her, wondering if she should go along with her plan that she came up with earlier. Paula felt Reader's stare, I h*ope she's not gay, cause I'm not with that.*

Reader decided to put her plan in motion. "Hey Paula. How serious are you and my peps?" Reader took a gulp of Don P straight from the bottle then passed it to Paula.

Paula took a gulp, "Girl me and Joey's cool and I'm feeling him a little but right now I'm just going with the flow. If we make it, we make it and if we don't, no love lost."

Reader stared on as Paula slurred and caught herself from falling out of her seat. Paula really liked Joey a lot but was not going to admit it that early in the relationship. Plus they haven't made any commitments so she kept her options open, just in case things didn't work out.

"Well Paula, we cool right?"

"Hell yea girl."

"So I can tell you anything right?"

"I'm all ears girl and stop beating around the bush and spit it out." Paula slurred and took another gulp of Don P.

"Ok then." Reader slurred, Girl I got a thing for Joey, dead serious, been this way since we were little kids. I dissed him in elementary school, I fucked up but things have since changed. Paula, I just wanted to let you know this because one day things might happen between me and Joey if he's willing but I don't want to lose your friendship over it. I mean he haven't given me indication that he's into me or nothing but if he's does, I'm not turning him down. So I'm letting you know what it is."

Paula laughed hard, busting a gut laughing at Reader.

"What you laughing for girl, I'm dead serious."

Paula continued to laugh then paused, "Girl I already knew that from when we were in the store where I used to work. I seen how you was watching him but I had just met him and it wasn't my place to step to you and even now it's not my place to step to you because me and Joey are not in a committed relationship. So if you're feeling him like that go for what you know. Hell I'll even back off girl."

Reader looked at Paula and squinted her eyes,

*Damn she don't give a fuck about Red.*

But Paula leaned in, "Listen Reader, don't think that I don't care about Joey. Its just that I know how men are. One minute they are sweet as cotton candy and the next they got that they want and you're history.

'Nah girl, Joey ain't like that. In fact I really think he's feeling you. And I don't want you to hurt him and in the process fuck up my chances of getting with him."

"Ok Reader. I'm hearing you and we cool so what you suggest that we do then?"

"Let's give that nigga the best of both worlds."

Paula confused about what Reader was suggesting, "What are you talking about?" She took another gulp of Don P and passed the bottle to Reader.

"We both can be his girl and he won't have time or room for any other bitches, feel me?"

"You crazy as hell Reader but you have a good point." Paula gave it some thought. "But what if he's not with it?"

"Girl look at us. We are the baddest bitches in this motherfucker. Who don't want us?

"Yea girl you're right, so how you want to go about it?"

Paula smirked cause her plan was in motion. "Like the real

bitches we are." Handing the Don P back to Paula.

"Ok I'm with it." Paula put the Don P to her mouth, "Bitch you done drunk the whole thing, order some more."

After ordering another bottle the ladies discussed how they were going to spring the good news on Joey while they go fucked up even more. Reader then pulled a blunt out of her purse, showing it to Paula.

"This shit here will get you all the way right." Reader pulled out a lighter.

"I don't smoke."

"You do tonight. I will never give you nothing that will hurt you. I love you sister." Reader stated drunk as hell with tears in her eyes and it was at that point Paula realized she had gained a true friend. The two women fired up the blunt, got high then started laughing at everything and everybody in the club.

- - - - -

D.J. T.J. Swan announced over the speakers, "Last call for alcohol." Dantwan, Lisa, Karen and A.J. made their way back to the VIP section. Tonya arrived about five minutes later still sipping on her Hypnotic. When Tyson and Joey finally arrived at the table everybody began gathering their things.

It was 4:45 A.M. and the club was winding down. Dantwan and Lisa was hugged up just before the family began walking towards the entrance of the club.

Big Willie spotted Joey and Tyson leaving, "Ok fellas I'll see y'all tomorrow night." As he looked at Reader, amazed that she was back to her old self, looking good because he was the one who turned her out.

"Yea we will give you a call and hopefully we can do business together." Joey replied.

"How you doing Reader?"

The family looked over at Reader wondering how they knew each other.

"Suck a dick bitch nigga." Reader was ready to slug him right where he stood.

The family stood quiet and Big Willie didn't jump down her throat because he noticed Reader was wearing the N.T.P family crest around her neck.

"Drive safe, Reader." Big Willie turned and walked out of the club.

Once the family got outside of the club, the Mayor spotted them, "Yo check it partner, it's some white boys over by your truck waiting on y'all." Pointing in the direction of their cars.

"Who are they?" Tyson asked figuring it was the police.

"Look like the Feds man." The Mayor replied stretching his eyes wide.

"A Mayor make sure Joey and his guest get to where they need to be. I heard that they are looking for him and I don't want nobody going to jail tonight, especially after having a good time. Tyson instructed.

"Holla at me tomorrow. I got something that I know you want." Tyson was referring to some weight that he would give the Mayor for the low.

"Aight. Joey follow me." Mayor led Joey to his car and told his number one hammer, Valentino to catch a ride to the hood with one of their runners.

Paula and Reader stood behind Joey and got in the back of Mayor's coup while Joey rode shotgun. The Mayor jumped in the car, turned the ignition then blast his music, knocking Run DMC, "Sucka MC's."

Everybody rode off in their cars as Joey looked at the white men talking to Tyson and Tonya standing by their truck.

"Excuse me sir, Is this one of your vehicles?" Agent Johnson asked Tyson who was walking towards one of the twin trucks with Tonya hanging on his arm.

"Yes, that's my wife's truck. Can we help you with anything, sir?"

Dantwan stood five feet away from them growling at the agent, helping Karen place A.J in the back seat of his truck.

Well we are looking for a Mr. Joey Knight and he was seen in this truck tonight. Do you know where he is?" Johnson asked as he looked inside the window.

"He was in the club but I believe he left with a woman earlier. Why what's the problem?

"Do you know what they are driving?" Johnson continued asking questions.

"No sir, I don't. Sorry I can't help you." Tyson replied looking at Tonya because she tugged his arm.

"Come on baby, I'm tired let's go home." Looking at him with a sexy smile ready to make love o him.

Tonya got into the truck while Dantwan and A.J. sat in the other truck with their ears glued on the conversation. Johnson then recognized A.J. from a photo in the files.

"How are you doing Mr. Jackson?" Johnson smiled at A.J.

"Hey man what's your motherfuckin' problem dog." Dantwan yelled from the driver's seat at Johnson.

"Got any drugs or guns in the car young man?" Johnson eyes Dantwan who had a nine millimeter in his hand ready to shoot the feds if he needed to.

"Yea a damn nuclear boom cracker."

"Watch the racial slurs nigger." Johnson shot back smiling.

Agent Johnson and Datwan stared at each other with hater in their eyes. Johnson knew if Joey Knight was a part of this crew then he wasting to be a big problem. So he broke the stare with Dantwan., "Look boy, don't drive drunk."

They knew as soon as Dantwan drove off, Johnson was going to pull him over. So Lisa took the wheel as Dantwan got in the passenger's seat. "You're right, sir." Then he turned his attention to Tyson. "Yo Ty, I'm out of here. I'll catch you tomorrow. Lisa crunk the car and drove off bumping, *"Fuck the Police.'*

"Ok sir, I apologize for holding you up. I can see your wife is ready to go home so I am going to let you leave. We need to question Joey Knight to clear up some matters. So if you see him before we do, please tell him to come talk to us before some road cop rolls up on him first, get my drift."

"Ok I'll personally see to it that he gets this information." Tyson replied getting into the truck, preparing to drive away when Dyson pulled up behind him.

Dyson lowered his window as he turned down his music, "Yo Ty?"

"Whats up cuz?" Tyson smiled ear to ear because he hasn't seen his cousin in a couple of months.

"Ain't no problem is it?"

"Hit me on the cell in about ten minutes. You got the number right?"

"Yeah I got it. I'll hit you in a minute." Dyson pulled off turning his system back up.

Tyson pulled out behind Dyson and they traveled down Airport road and came out on 291 South Pleasantburg drive.


When Dyson and Tyson drove off Agent Johnson turned to one of his agents, "Them boys think they are slick but they will slip up and we will get them, trust me."

"Get them for what sir?" One of the younger agents asked.

"For breathing and breading others like hem."

# CHAPTER 29

As the Mayor escorted Paul, Reader, and Joey to Joey's condo he had just purchased, the two women kept responding Joey as daddy during the conversation. Reader and Paula was still intoxicated and high. Joey kept looking back at them in the back seat, not knowing what as going on with them. Although he figured that they had a little too much to drink. Reader and Paula starting teasing Joey to get him horny for the both of them.

Reader was sitting directly behind Joey so she reached her hand around the passenger side seat and pinched him on the ass. Joey damn near jumped out of his seat as the girls laughed.

"Damn boy, you got it going on nigga." The Mayor looked through his rearview at the women.

"Nah partner, it ain't like that, their drunk."

"Oh hell yea it is like that." Reader stated.

"Believe that." Paula chimed in and the men laughed.

After a few more minutes of touching and teasing Joey, the Mayor pulled into a subdivision, full of condos on the East side of Greenville. He pulled up in a parking space then grabbed his phone off his hip and pressed speed dial. The phone rung three times before Tyson answered.

"Yeah tell it."

"He's home safe and sound."

"Is Reader still with y'all?"

"Yeah she's back there drunk. Mayor replied as Joey got out of the car.

"Let me speak with her."

"Reader, phone."

Reader took the put the phone to her ear, "Yeah."

"How's it going?"

"Hey Ty, everything is going accordingly to plan. But if you don't let us finish it will never work."

"Girl you just horny and drunk, I'll holla at you later. Put Mayor back on the phone.

Reader handed Mayor back the phone and Tyson let him know that he'll get at him tomorrow. Mayor disconnected the phone as he watched the ladies play sexual games with Joey, "Yo Red you sure you don't want me to stay for a little while?"

"Nah, he got this nigga, kick wheels." Reader chimed in and Joey bust out laughing.

"Oh shit it's like that Reader?"

"Nigga I'm just fucking wth you. Stop taking shit so serious." Reader replied as she adjusted her dress which had crawled up her legs showing her thick thighs.

Joey began walking to his condo with both women under his arms as Mayor drove off thinking about how he would have Reader in all kinds of positions if she let him. Joey let loose of the girls and made a dash for his condo to lock the girls out because he knew what they were up to, at least, he thought he did. He thought that Paula was trying to test him since she had seen him looking at Reader on their way to the club and he didn't want to get caught up in their little game.

However Reader being he track star, kicked off her high hills and ran Joey down before he could get to the door. Paula picked up Reader's heels and walked to the door where Reader was holding Joey by the arm. Paula laughing along with Joey and Reader, "Now you know you should have not tried that. You know it's on now." Smiling a devilish smile.

Reader removed the keys from Joey's pocket and opened the door while Joey tried to keep them out. But the women paid him no attention. Once the door was open they shoved Joey inside and slammed the door behind him.

- - - - -

After Chop and Mark left the club, Mark began calling Chop all types of bitches and punk motherfuckas because he let Mayor pimp slap him in front of everybody. Mark fresh out of jail, was realizing that not only the game changed but the people in the game changed too. Power, respect, and money was they key aspects of the game more than anything.

Mark didn't even care about the fact that Chop came to get him out of jail, put clothes on his back, money in his pocket, fed him like he was one of his own kids, and on top of that go him some of the best pussy that was offered to a man, cause he'd lost all respect for Chop.

"Where you going man." Chop had heard enough of Mark's verbal abused as he rode down Ackley road in Nichol Town then made a left turn onto Rebecca Street.

"What nigga?"

"I said, where you going?

"You a bitch ass nigga. Stay the fuck away from me, for I fuck you up nigga." Mark replied as Chop pulled over at the Dirton number spot. He got out, slamming the door, cursing as Chop drove off. Mark stood there in the middle of the street half drunk around five o'clock in the morning as he heard loud thumping, car stereo music playing a few blocks over. He began walking towards the block where he saw five older guys standing on the corner. He decided to head in their direction. The guys were a bunch crack dealers who smoked their own product. They sold crack to feed their own habits. Even though these old school hustlers smoked crack, they knew how to get their paper, rain, sleet hail or snow.

Mark walked passed them to go sit on the steps of the Delia night club in the heart of Nichol town. He watched the old hustlers clock dollars. Mark reached down in his pocket and realized that he only had thirty-five dollars to his name. He thought that while he was at the club, he should have made Chop pay for all the drinks. Then he thought that he should have never bought them two girls drinks that he met at the bar. He knew that out of his thirty- five dollars, ten would go to cab fair to get across town to his mothers house. They had previously go into an argument which ended in her kicking him out he house along with Mike. He vowed then that he would never go back  but with no where to g, he had no other choice. As Mark sat there on the steps contemplating his next move and watching the hustlers getting money, he noticed an Escalade truck, pull up. It looked like the same truck he seen parked at the club earlier.

After the truck stopped, Dantwan jumped out and two of the old hustlers reached into their pockets and handed him knots of money. Dantwan then went to the back of the truck and pulled out a black back pack and handed them with more product. Mark noticed a girl in the front seat and another in the back sitting with A.J.. Dantwan tossed the back pack back in the truck and ran around the driver side and jumped back in. Mark watched as Dantwan drove off knocking R. Kelly's, 'Bmp and Grind.' One of the old timers walked over to Mark,

"What's happening young blood, you look familiar." Making sure to get a close look at Mark in case he was a stick up kid.

"Aint nothing happening. Just tired as a motherfucka."

"Go home and get some rest then."

Mark looked at Tuna crazy but brushed off Tuna's reply as he got up and began walking down the street towards the fairway. Half way down the four way, a car passed by Mark and waved it down trying to catch a ride. The car stopped and Mark took off jogging towards the car. As Mark approached the beat up Escort two guys was in the car. One of the guys stuck his head out of the window, "What's popping homie?"

The two cats in the car were stick up kids. Their plan was to rob Mark. They had seen the old hustler Tuna, talking to Mark and was hoping that he gave him some money or that Mark was going to pick it up so when Mark left they followed him.

"What you need a ride, where you going?" One of the boys asked looking at Marks pocket and gold chain around his neck that belonged to Chop.

"Yeah I need a ride." Mark got into the car.

As the three began riding, Mark noticed that the driver of the car kept watching him through the rearview mirror. Mark had seen this cats eyes before but couldn't remember where.

"Meatball." Thought they said he got killed a year ago, Mark said.

Meatball began looking harder at Mark and realized it was one of his old homies from Washington Street. Mark's mother lived on Washington Street where meatball was raised. They used to play together as kids until they came of age and went different ways. Meatball also remembered that Mark had went to jail some time back.

"What's going on my nigga, when you get out?"

"Shit yesterday.I didn't think you would realize it was me back here.

The other dude sitting in the passenger street turned around to look at Mark to get a better look at him.

"So what them niggas been up to down the road." Meatball remembered that a year ago when he caught his sixty day sentence, he had ran into Mark at the bus terminal during an institutional transfer.

Mark made a couple of remarks about the guys that was servicing time down the road but he shifted his conversation to Chop and the incident that happened at the club. After Mark had mentioned the Mayors name Meatball and his partner knew who he was talking about but neither one of them cared about the Mayor or anybody else for that matter.

After hearing about how much of a bitch Chop was made a clever statement, "We should ride that bitch nigga tonight before the sunrise." Firing up a Newport.

"Shid we can do that, what he going to do." Mark replied.

"You know where he live at?"

"Somewhere in Berea. I know how to get there." Mark smiled thinking about how he was getting ready to make a come up.

"Let's roll then." Meatball made a U-turn in the middle of the street. "Mark this is my main man Yellow boy. He used to love over here in Nicholtown.

Yellow boy looked like he was skid up on something strong but Mark replied, "Yea I remember him around here but it was a long time ago.

Mark reached for the Newport that Meatball was handing to him as they rode towards Chops crib to rob him.

- - - - -

"Will y'all stop!" Joey yelled grabbing Reader's hand from his mid section.

"Daddy don't want to have no fun." Reader said in a soft baby voice while Paula tried to undue his pants.

"Hold up y'all, let's sit down and talk about this."

"And have sex." Reader added causing Joey to laugh.

"For real. Now stop!" Joey said as he slapped Reader's hand away from his manhood.

Paula saw that Joey was serious so she stopped playing around. Joey looked at Paula, "How do you feel about this?"

"Look Joey, me and Reader already talked about this. And we decided that to keep our friendship, we should share you together than to be against each other.

"But I haven't been fucking with Reader on that lever and for good reasons too. We're partners." Joey gave Reader a stern look letting her know that she knew better. But what he didn't know was that it was Tyson who called the shot.

"Well Joey things change and you're fucking with me now. Reader replied grabbing Joeys hand as Paula grabbed the other hand.

"Because she has always loved you and I have fallen in love with you too. Paula added.

"So you with this Paula, are you sure?"

"It's whatever you want daddy. Plus I've never done a threesome."

Reader then walked up behind Joey and began rubbing his shoulders while Paula leaned in to kiss him. Reader then began licking on Joeys neck as Paula unbuttoned his silk shirt. As Reader rubbed Joeys shoulders he moaned as Reader dug into his tensed muscles. Reader then walked around the couch and stat on the other side of Joey. Paula began unbuttoning his belt and pants and then the two ladies slid them off of him.

Paula then grabbed Joey's pole, stroking it up and down with her hand while Reader kissed him all over his chest. As Paula streaked him reader guided her tongue down his chest to his mid section until she reached his the tip of his manhood, placing her tongue on it as Paula held it. Reader sucked the tip of his head as Joey closed his eyes and moaned. Reader and Paula took turned sucking and licking Joey's love muscle while they played with his nuts. After sucking and licking the girls got off their knees and walked into Joey's master bedroom, undressing while they looked back at Joey.

Joey stood up from the couch with a full erection, thinking to himself how lucky he was at this moment. Joey took of the rest of his clothes and proceeded towards his bedroom. When he got into his room, the women pulled him down on the bed. The two began sucking his manhood again. Then Reader mounted Joey allowing the head of his dick to enter her tight wet pussy. Reader gasp for air as Joey's manhood ripped through her tight pussy. Reader hadn't had sex in over nine months and being with Joey seems as if it was her first time having sex. Joey pumped his hips as he pushed his manhood all the way in and Reader screamed, "Ohhh Joey." Freezing in position from the pleasure of pain.

The pain and pleasure caused Readers nipples to harden. Paula positioned herself on top of Joey's face, placing her pussy in his mouth. Joey began eating Paula and thrusting his hips into Reader. The two women rolled their asses around in slow motion pleasing Joey and letting him please them. They all moaned in satisfaction.

Reader moaned, "Daddy I'm coming!"

Followed by Paula moaning, "Papi It's coming!"

Joey began eating and thrusting faster and aggressively. The two women then came hard. Cream from Paula's pussy leaked all over Joey's mouth while the cream from Reader's pussy was all over his mid section. Joey had not came yet and was fining for his nut.

Reader then motioned to Paula to sit down on Joey's manhood with her ass towards his face. Reader licked all of Joey's chest as Paula rode him like a wild cowgirl.

"Ooh Papi. Ooh, I'm coming!" As she summed harder than the first time.

Reader told Paula to move aside. She was determined to make Joey come in her.

"Fuck me daddy. Please fuck me good." Reader flipped Joey on top of her body.

Joey grabbed Readers legs and placed them on his forearm and shoved his dick into her, pumping slow and easy. Paula laid there watching and smiling. Reader then grabbed Joey's dick from under her leg and pulled it out of her pussy and put the head at the entrance of her anus. Joey rammed into her ass like it was her pussy. Reader screams like a white mouth mule, "Oooh! As Joey slowed his stroke down.

Joey continued the strokes as Reader began using her ass muscles driving Joey out of his mind. Reader then grabbed his dick and pushed it back into her pussy. Joey pumped harder as Reader rolled her hips, tightened her pussy muscles, and lifted her ass to make his dick reach the bottom of her pussy. His back arched and he moaned as he came inside of her.

They flopped down sweating like they had just go finished working out in the gym. Joey rolled off Reader and the two women laid on his chest and soon fell asleep.

# CHAPTER 30

Mark, Meatball, and yellow boy pulled up on a side street in Berea and walked through a wooded path, which led to Chop's house. Mark noticed Chop car sitting infant of his house. The sun was coming up and they only had a couple of minutes before it would be daylight. So they planned to make the quick robbery and get out of there. Mark and his new friends walked up to the from door. Mark knocked on the door while the other two stood on the side of the door so that Chop couldn't see them out of the peep hole.

"Who is it?" Chop yelled, wondering who could be knocking on his door at this hour.

"Mark man."

"Hold up one second, I'll be right there."

Chop went to the back bedroom and opened his closet, and grabbed his two twin seventeen shot blocks before heading back to the door. Chop knew that Mark was a dirty nigga so he was going to be prepared for nay bullshit Mark tried to pull. Chop walked to the door and unlocked it slowly so Mark couldn't hear the click sound from the lock. Then he backed away from the door and laid on his belly with the twin clocks pointing at the door.

"The door is open man." Aiming perfectly at his target.

Meatball and Yellow boy rushed past Mark into Chop's house with their guns drawn and was met by several slugs. One slug caught Yellow boy in the eye and another one in his throat. Meatball caught two slugs in the chest and one in the neck. The two men hit the floor as Chop keep his aim at the front door. He began walking slowly towards the door where Mark stood frozen, scared for his life.

"Yo homie them nigga's kidnapped me and made me bring them headman. They been watching us all night." Dropping his head to his chest unable to look Chop in the eyes.

Chop reached over and snatched his chain off Marks neck, "Shut the fuck up bitch nigga." Grabbing Mark by the back of the neck putting one of the clocks to his head. He led Mark into his house then spun Mark to the floor.

Chop stood over Mark while he curled up on the floor with one hand reaching out towards Chop's glock begging for his life. Chop heard one of the other men moaning in pain so he turned towards the body and fired two slugs into him. he then pointed the gun back at Mark,

"Nigga I knew you was coming. You ungrateful piece of shit."

'It aint like that man. I swear."

"Shut the fuck up nigga. Now who's acting like a bitch."

While Chop talked shit to Mark, Meatball laid behind him in a pool of blood, dying a slow death. But with every ounce of strength he had left, he raised his gun, which fell like a ton, fired a shot. The slug hit Chop right in the mouth just as he was about to say something else to Mark. The bullet went straight through his mouth and came out the back of his head, killing him instantly. Chop's body fell down to the floor and at the same time, Meatball took his last breath.

Mark was the last man standing. He looked around at the room full of dead bodies, *Oh God let me get the fuck out of here.* He rushed to the front door then stopped in his tracks. *Hell ain't no need in leaving empty handed, this nigga dead.*

Mark remembered the bay safe that Chop showed him earlier so he ran to the bathroom and opened the closet. Lucky for him the safe was open because Chop also hid his guns in the safe and wasn't planning on dying. Mark took the stack of hundred and the stack of twenty dollar bills. He ran back into the living room and looked out the window to see if anybody was coming. Then he grabbed a black back pack off the couch on his way back to the bathroom. He emptied the contents of the safe into the bag and was preparing to leave the house until he saw the bedroom. The bedroom door was slightly opened so he stepped in and saw four pounds of marijuana sitting on the floor in the corner of the room. Chop also had 18 ounces of cocaine on his dresser. Mark felt like he hit the jack pot. He scooped up all the drugs placing it into the back pack and left.

Children were running to catch the school bus while old people were looking in his direction. Mark ran around the house and headed towards Meatballs car. He heard sirens heading towards Chops direction as he reached the car. He hoped into the car and took off. He sung in excitement, smiling ear to ear because he'd just made a sweet come up. He made his way to the Motel Six and rented a room. Once in the room he tossed the bag under the bed and laid on the bed thinking about everything that happened over the last 24 hours. Reader's face invaded his thoughts. It soon after he remembered where he remembered her from,

*Crackhead from the bricks.*

- - - - -

Reader jumped up out of her sleep, "Mark!" Causing Paula and Joey to wake up.

"What's wrong baby?" Joey asked.

Reader told Joey that she remember who the guy is that her and Paula was arguing with at the club. Joey then told Paula to grab his phone. Joey called Tyson who in return called for a meeting at the Safe Haven at 10:00 A.M. on the dot.

"What time is it?" Joey asked Reader.

"8:45 baby."

"Well I got about an hour to waste so what the two prettiest women in Greenville gone do for daddy?" Smiling with an early morning hard on.

"I thought you'd never asked. Reader replied as she positioned herself on top of Joey and Paula soon followed.

- - - - -

Dantwan was awaken by Lisa kissing his lips and handing him his cell phone.

"Yeah tell it." Sitting up in bed.

"We have a meeting at 10 sharp. Safe Haven."

The phone disconnected then Dantwan slung the phone to the wall and turned over, pulling the covers back over his head. Five minutes later Lisa returned handing him his phone again. Dantwan looked at her like he wanted to kill her. She rolled her eyes and sucked her teeth before heading back to the kitchen to continue cooking breakfast.

"Yeah."

"It's 9:15, get your ass up now." Tyson disconnected the call again.

Tyson knew that Dantwan was going to turn over and go right back to sleep the first time he called. But this time he removed the cover and got up cussing under his breath. Dantwan walked into Lisa's guest room where Karen and A.J. slept. He caught Karen ass mounted on top of A.J.

"Hurry up A.J. we got a meeting at ten sharp." And walked back out of the room as Karen jumped off A.J. covering her body with her hands.

Dantwan went into the bathroom and got into the shower, brushed his teeth, and got dressed as quick as he could. Karen helped A.J. bathe and get dressed and by 9:45 they were headed out of the door. They got into A.J.'s new whip and pulled off. The entire NT family arrived at the Safe Haven at the same time.

- - - - -

After Joey and Reader left for the meeting, Paula caught a cab to her town house to check on things. She turned on her answering machine to listen to her messages while she packed her clothes because she planned on staying at Joey's for a few more days. There was three messages on her answering machine. The first message was from her boss at the Citgo letting her know she can return to work and would be receiving a raise. The second message was from the family attorney requesting she call him immediately and the million dollar insurance check from Pedro's death cleared and has been mailed to her uncle's house. The third message was from Sara letting her know that her check arrived and that Gormez wanted to see her.

Paula sat back on her bed and began thinking about everything that happened last night and how much she enjoyed herself at the club and her first threesome. She wondered how it felt when Joey stuck his dick in Reader's ass, thinking she should try it one day.

Paula grabbed the remote control and turned on the T.V just in time to catch the news. The reporter was standing outside a town house showing three dead bodies being loaded onto a meat wagon. The reporter announced the names of the victims showing a picture of them as well. Paula's mouth dropped wide when Chop's picture was shown on the screen. *That's that guy that called me a drunk bitch at the club.* She wondered if Mark had anything to do with it but didn't give it much thought. Instead she picked up the phone to call her uncle.

After three Mexican men dressed in all black raided the safe house, Shantez was moved from Idaho and given another new name and location. Word around the station was that a mole was in the department. Shantez often thought about backing out of the deal with the federal government being that he lived looking over his shoulder at all times. But he decided that he would ride the snitch mobile to the end of the road and if God had mercy on his he would live through it and perhaps one day write a book about his life.

"Mr. Shantez get your belongings." One of the federal agents yelled removing his gun from his holster.

"Why?" Shantez asked because he had just settled in the new location.

"We have received a tip that the location has been leaked again, so hurry up and let's move now!"

Shantex grabbed a couple of things and followed the agents to the front door. One agent went out the door first to make sure the surroundings was clear. He saw a van pulling up as his phone begin ringing

"Yes sir." The agent answered.

"Move now, they have found your location." The voice on the other end yelled.

The agents began rushing Shantez out the front door into the small van that pulled up in front of the safe house. The agent that received the call thought that voice on the other end was agent Patterson but it wasn't. It was the mole in the department. As the van pulled off, ten Mexicans came out of nowhere and began unloading automatic weapons. The bullets hit the van.

Agent Patterson was on his way to the safe house and showed up as the Mexicans were unloading bullets into the van. Patterson ran his vehicle into the car that was blocking the Van carrying Shantez. Two of the agents in the van were slumped over dead while Shantez was shaking like a leaf on a windy fall day in the back of the van.

"Stay down Shantez!" Agent Patterson yelled as he entered the driver's side of the van, pulling the dead body from the van to the ground. He got into the van and put the pedal to the metal and pulled off. Rubber was burning leaving a cloud of smoke behind. The Mexican's jumped into their cars and began chase, still firing their weapons. Bullets busted outage back window of the van. Patterson reached down in his leg holster and pulled out a gun, tossed it to Shantez, "If you want to live, use it."

Shantez began firing back at the Mexicans but it wasn't long before he ran out of ammo. Patterson was a yard ahead of the Mexicans and made a sharp right turn and stopped the van. "Get out now. Go into the building right there with the red dot on it. Someone else will pick you up, now go."

Patterson drove off, grabbing his radio requesting back up. The Mexicans pulled up behind him firing their weapons. They shot out two tires, causing the van to fishtail and flip, throwing Patterson twenty feet away into a ditch. The Mexicans rushed the van and began unloading their guns. Another Mexican agent then came running and attached some C-4 explosive to the gas tank, holding the detonator in his other hand.

Patterson rose from the ditch and began firing two Desert Eagles killing some of the Mexicans surrounding the van. The other Mexicans turned around firing at Patterson. Seconds later federal agents surrounded the area. The Mexicans took off running disappearing into thin air, leaving the explosives in place. Federal agents carefully approached the van and begin searching it. Once the Mexicans were out of the agents view, pressed the detonator and the van exploded killing the agents. The other agents moved for cover as the van sat burning. Agent Johnson then pulled up after the explosive and walked over towards Agent Patterson.

"What happened here?"

"We received a call informing us to move out the safe house."

"No one in the department called. We have a serious problem, a fucking mole."

"Where is the witness?"

"I followed protocol and dropped him off at the building with he red dot."

"Come on we got to move fast." They ran towards Johnson's vehicle.

# CHAPTER 31

The NTP family sat around the round table at the Safe Haven. Tyson wanted to make sure that everybody had handled their business so that they could get the situation behind them and began to live a care free life again.

"What's the line of business for todays meeting." Tyson asked the table.

"Well I think everybody should know that nigga, Reader and Paula got into with at the club was Mike Wilson's little brother, Mark.

"I thought I seen him sitting on Delisa steps let night ." A,J. added.

So what do you think we should do about Mark but before you answer that allow me to show you something first." Tyson grabbed the remote control and turned on the T.V., displaying the news he recorded earlier showing Chop, Meatball, and Yellow boy.

"That's that motherfucker that was with Mark last night."

"Yea I know I received a call from the Mayor early this morning. I asked him to look into it." Tyson directed the family's attention back to the news reporter.

"I think we should body his ass." Dantwan replied, with malice in his heart.

"It's better safe than sorry." A.J. added.

"Any objections?" Tyson asked.

"Yea I think we should wait a little longer because we might not have to get our hands dirty at all. The police might snatch him for the murders or kill them for us. Joey explained and Reader agreed.

"That sounds good to me. Does everybody agree with Joey?" Tyson asked.

The family looked around at one another then all agree with Joey's idea.

"Speaking of the police, Joey you need to go down town to talk to Agent Johnson about the murder of Mike Wilson. If you don't go they will come looking for you so get your story together." Tyson instructed.

"I'll go with him." Reader replied with her hand under the table rubbing Joey's leg.

"Joey I called in a favor from my cousin, an O.G in the game, and he gave me a name and number for you to call, Ms Debra. So call her before you go downtown and she will make sure you're alright." Tyson looked around the table, "Anything else?"

"Yea, Big Willie." Joey asked.

"Well I'm going to see him while you're downtown handling your business. I got that handled."

Tyson announced the meeting adjourned.

- - - - -

"Hello Gomez Residence, may I help you?" Sara answered the

phone.

"Hey Sara, this Paula. Sorry it's taken me so long to return your phone call."

"How are you doing baby? You need to come to the ranch immediately."

"Why? Is there something wrong?"

"Your uncle is very ill. The doctor doesn't know how much time he has left."

"I'll be right there." Paula hung up grabbing her car keys.

Paula walked out her front door to her car and 45 minutes later she was at Mr. Gormez's house. Gormez's bodyguard stopped Paula at the front door. He stepped aside as soon as he recognized who she was.

"Sara!" Paula yelled out as she walked through the house.

"I'm back here, Paula." Sara yelled from the back room of the house sitting behind Gormez's desk.

Paula proceeded through the house to Gormez's office.

"Where's Papa?" Paula asked wondering why Sara was sitting behind her uncles desk.

"Sit down Paula, we need to talk."

Paula took a seat and stared at Sara hoping she wasn't giving her bad news.

"Paula your uncle wants to see you immediately." Standing up from behind the desk.

"Where is he?"

"He's in Mexico. A private jet is waiting for you at the air port. He is expecting you in the next three hours." Walking from behind the desk motioning with her hands to one of the bodyguards to take

Paula to the airport.

While on the private jet, Paula called Joey's cellphone but didn't get an answer so she left a voicemail to let him know that she would be gone for a few hours due to family illness. She also ended her message, "I had a beautiful time last night."

- - - - -

One of Mr. Gormez lieutenants named Heinz was sitting in a Taco Bell waiting on his runners. Heinz had three major runners in South Carolina; Charleston, Columbia, and Greenville. As he sat in the Taco Bell staring out the window a blue Expedition truck pulled into the parking lot. A big guy weighing over three hundred pounds, standing at 6'2 stepped out of the truck. Big Willie was wearing all blue matching the color of his truck. He also had on a huge platinum iced out chain. He walked into the Taco Bell and looked around at the people occupying the tables before he spotted Heinz sitting by the window.

Heinz was sipping on his soda as the big guy walked over to his table. "Sit down." Keeping his eyes on the newspaper that he was reading.

"What you reading about?" Big Willie sat down.

"Nothing. Have you heard anything on the streets about Mr. Gormez heroin yet?"

"I thought the police got the heroin out of the shooting gallery when they found Tony dead."

"Come on big man, you can't be that fucking slow. You know damn well the police lied about confiscating that much heroin. We got people posted in the station that verify that the heroin is still on the streets. So what I need you to do is find out who got it."

"Well I'll keep my eyes and ears open and contact you if I find something in a couple of days."

Heinz then stood up and shook Big Willie's hand before leaving the Taco Bell in a brown pick up truck. Big Willie got into his truck and headed to meet Tyson and Joey to see what type of business proposal they were trying to make.

- - - - -

Shantez was no where to be found when Agent Johnson and Patterson went to the building he left him at.

"Where is he at?" Johnson asked.

"This is where I told him to come, following protocol. I told him that someone will be to pick him up.

"Well he's not here."

"Don't you think I see that."

Both agents gave each other a cold stare down.

"Let's get out of here." Johnson ordered.

They didn't know that Shantez was picked up by Gormez's men when he entered the building. In fact the mole knew all about the emergency protocol drop off. Gomez had slipped bak into the country for the sole purpose of murdering Shantez. Gormez's men hogged tide Shantez to a chair with sharp wires. Every time he moved the wires would cut deep into his skin. While Gomez men waited on him to arrive they slapped, punched, and kicked Shantez to kill time.

Gomez showed up an hour later with Shantez's mother, who

was once married to Gomez some years back but now divorced. But he still fucked her whenever he wanted to so she was easy to reach. Gomez and Peggy stood for him as Shantez raised his head, blood running down the side of his face from the gash in his head.

"You disappoint me Shantez."

Shantez tried to raise his amputated hand and was slapped by his mother as she yelled, "You are a disgrace to the entire family. I should've aborted you." She spit in Shantez's face.

Shantez looked up at this mother and step father and started laughing. His mother's lost love and words of disappointment tormented him mentally, shattered his world and darkened his heart. He gathered enough saliva in his mouth and spit on Gormez, "You go to hell bastard."

Mr. Gormez looked down at his taylor made suit and shook his head, "You should have spit on the police when they questioned you. And as to going to hell, you first." Gormez motioned for his men. As Gomez and Peggy walked off the men tortured Shantez as ordered. They did things to him that no one would believe.

# CHAPTER 32

Joey and Reader showed up at Ms. Debra Butler and Associates Law Firm on 209 Chapman Street in downtown Greenville. They walked into the building to the receptionist desk. She ordered them to head to the back. Joey and Reader knocked on the Ms. Debra's office and a soft elevate voice from the other side announced, "Please come on in and take a seat."

Joey and Reader entered and sat in a big leather chairs that sate before Ms. Butler's desk. Ms. Butler was on the phone when they entered. She motioned with her hand that she would be with them in a moment. While Joey and Reader sat in Ms. Butler's office why began looking around at her office and noticed all kinds of law journals and books. then they saw a picture of Ms. Butler and an old black man who looked like he was in the mafia. He had his hand around Ms. Butler like they are the best of friends. Next to that picture was another picture with her and a young black brother who looked familiar. Joey and Reader knew they recognized the brother from the club the other night. Joey noticed he wore a medallion around his neck with the NTP crest then remembered that it was Dyson, Tyson's cousin. Dyson barely hung around the hood anymore unless he came through and shot some basketball or a block party cookout

"I'll be with y'all in one minute. We running late." Ms. Debra hung up the phone and grabbed a book from the shelf. As she rambled through the book and found what she was looking for, she wrote it down then closed the book.

"Joey Knight, right?" Extending a hand to Joey and Reader.

"Yes Ma'am, I'm Joey Knight."

"Well y'all ready to go?" Debra asked stepping from behind her desk walking towards the office door.

Joey and Reader got up from the chairs and followed Debra out of the building.

"We will take my car."

Joey, Reader and Debra got into her 500xl Benz and she drove to the old Federal Building. They entered the double doors and a security guard sate at the desk with two guards standing by the entrance. The security guard at the desk spoke to Ms. Debra.

"Hey, Ms. Butler, haven't seen you in a while." Tilting his hat to her.

"How are you doing Frank?" Debra smiled.

"What can I do for you?"

"We have a meeting with Agent Johnson."

"Please go down to the other desk, they will guide you in the right direction."

"Thank you Frank."

The three of them walked through another set of double doors, entering an office. A circled shaped desk sat in the middle of the office with three clerks sitting behind the desk.

"We're here to see Agent Johnson."

"Please hold for one-second." The clerk replied while checking some files, "What's your name?"

"Joey Knight." Debra answered for her client.

"I'm sorry Ms. Butler but Agent Johnson is out on assignment and won't be back for at least four hours but Agent Sims is here and can assist you.

"We will be happy to talk to Agent Sims and thank you."

"Would y'all please follow me."

Joey, Reader, and Debra followed the clerk to Agent Sims office not knowing that Sim's was Gormez's mule. Once sitting in front of Sims Debra felt something wasn't right when Sim's didn't seem to know why Joey was meeting with Agent Johnson.

"Well if you don't know why we need to be questioned about and we don't know what we need to be questioned about then maybe we made a mistake. But we were hoping you could fill us in."

"Well I don't know what this is about but if you leave your name and number, I'll have Agent Johnson give you a call when he returns."

"Thank you very much for your time." Debra stated standing up.

Debra shook Sims hand and then proceeded to walk out of Sim's office with Reader and Joey following behind her. They reached the hall of the front entrance.

"See you later, Ms. Butler." Frank smiled.

"Alright Frank, take care of yourself.

The three hoped in Debra's car and just before she pulled off she asked if they were hungry.

"Sure we can use something to eat." Joey replied.

"Good cause I'm starving." She applied some lip gloss and smacked her lips together, "I have to meet a friend at the cafe, every Thursday, it's Thursday right?"

"Yea it's Thursday." Reader responded.

"Well, let's just go meet my friend at the cafe and grab something to eat."

Debra road around for ten minutes, taking the long way to the cafe. She parked across the street from the cafe and they sat in the car for a few minutes before getting out. They watched as white people with suits and briefcases entered and exited the cafe. They walked to the entrance and was greeted by the waitress.

"How are you doing today, Ms. Butler, your normal table?"

"Yes please." Debra looked around the cafe for her friend.

"Follow me please." The waitress escorted them to their table.

- - - - -

Mark was awaken by pounding on the motel room door. It was a maid letting him know that it was check out time. Mark jumped out the bed still fully dressed and grabbed the book bag from under the bed. he exited the room and walked down the hallway of the motel. he noticed a couple of guys that was at the club the night before checking out of the hotel with a bunch of women. They all looked like they had been up for weeks with no sleep. Mark walked to the motel lobby and used a pay phone to call a cab and left Meatball's escort in the parking lot.

"Where to sir?"

"Take me to the Holiday Inn on 291 on Pleasantburg Drive."

Ten minutes later he arrived at the hotel and paid his cab driver. He walked into the hotel and rented a room. He emptied the contents of the book bag onto the bed and began counting the money and breaking down the drugs as best he could, without a scale. He counted out seventy-five thousand dollars in cash. He decided to take a shower then called another cab to pick him up. The cab driver arrived ten minutes later blowing his horn.Mark ran out of the hotel and jumped into the cab.

"Drop me off at Haywood Mall."

The cab driver turned on his meter and began driving. Mark left the mall fresh to death an hour later. He caught another cab back to the hotel. This time he had the driver wait while he rushed into the hotel room and grabbed three ounces of cocaine and an ounce of marijuana.

"Head to Nichol town."

Mark paid his tab and got out on the block in Nichol town. He saw few youngsters chasing down cars to sell crack. Mark walked to an empty house and dug a small hole. He put his dope in the hole and covered it up. Mark stood about twenty feet away from the hole and watched the youngsters and crack heads for about an hour before he made his move. He knew that he was in someone else's territory and knew it was most likely Dantwan's. So he decided to run his dope through the young runners.

"Yo young blood."

"What's popping blood."

"Ain't much what y'all doing out here."

"Shit waiting for our peeps to come back through so we can re-up." Sperm head replied, not knowing if he was talking to an undercover or jack boy. So Mark knew it would be easy to dump his product.

"Well how much you got? I'll double whatever you got?"

"I got enough for a quarter spoon. And I got two more people who want half an ounce each."

Mark told lil sperm head to go get his money and come back. Dude rand off running and ten minutes later he returned with thirteen hundred dollars.

"Bless me." Handing Mark the money with his hand on his twenty-five automatic.

"What's wrong partner?"

"Just making sure you don't try no slick shit with my money." Sperm head replied looking serious.

"Don't worry about that, hold your money and I'll be right back." Mark dashed behind the empty house to retrieve his stash and came back with an ounce and a half. While Mark was making his transaction, an old timer, named Tuna, watched. Tuna works for Dantwan so he grabbed his cell phone and dialed Dantwans number and was instructed to keep an eye on Mark.

# CHAPTER 33

Tyson moved through traffic coming down White Horse Road on his way to meet with Big Willie. He made a left and jumped on East Faris Road and put the pedal to the metal looking through his rearview mirror. As Tyson drove he wondered if Joey knew about his plot with Reader. He wanted Paula close to the family so that he could use her as a bargaining chip if he needed to.

Tyson had surfed the internet and got information on Paula and found out the she was related to Gomez. He also found out that the Gomez family went to war with the Gararos. He also found out that a member of the Gararos family named Ricka was forced out of Mexico by the five families because he lost the war. Ricka was now associated with the Italian Mafia and still pushing heroin in Florida. Tyson made a couple of phone calls down to Florida while during his research and asked his people did they know him. They didn't know him but knew people who could get in touch with him. Tyson had his people contact Ricka for a key and a half of raw heroin. being that Ricka was struggling he immediately jumped on it.

Tyson then made a left turn and was riding up the Motor Mile. He made a right and pulled up into Gower Park and parked his car.

A female softball game was going on. Thirty-seconds later Big Willie pulled up and parked his car as Tyson was getting out of his. The two men greeted each other, shaking hands and began walking through the park.

"So what's up Tyson. I know you ain't got me out here about pulling no licks?"

"It is to my understanding the you're supplying half of Greenville with that dog food."

"What the fuck is going on man?" Big Willie asked because he never discussed drugs with Tyson before.

"Chill Will, If we are going to do business, I'm going to be straight with you and you don't have worry about me being the police. If you think that I'd murk your ass right here. Is that real enough for ya." Tyson looked Big Willie directly in the eyes.

"Thats what they all say at first."

They stared at each other wondering if they should do business with each other. However Tyson needed Big Willie so that his plan would work. Tyson then broke the silence,

"Look man, everything straight. I need to know how much you are paying for a key."

Big Willie didn't respond right away thinking, *Ty is green as a mothafucka because even the police wouldn't be this direct.* "I get a brick for ten thousand if I am buying over fifty of them things."

"You're misunderstanding me, Will. I am talking about a brick of heroin."

Big Willie's eyes got big. *I wonder if this who Heinz looking for.* "It all depends, whether its raw or uncut."

"In the purest form."

Big Willie put one and one together and came up with two. This nigga trying to sell me Gormez's dope. I wonder if I should turn him in.

"For raw heroin, I pay eighty-five thousand but the going rate tis one hundred twenty-five thousand for pure."

Well check this out. I got a man who wants to get rid of a brick and a half of raw heroin for one hundred thousand. And it can go for twelve."

Big Willie knew then that this was indeed Gormez's product because he was the only one with raw heroin that can stand a twelve easy. For a quick moment Big Willie contemplated whether he should cop the heroin and sell it without Heinz knowing about it since it's the same product that Heinz gives him anyway. But he quickly dismissed that thought.

"Ty hold up a minute let me peps to get the money together." He stepped away from Tyson and called Heinz. "I believe I found your guy." Big Willie looked over his shoulders at Tyson.

"Set up the deal and call me with the time and location."

Big Willie closed his cellphone and walked back over to Tyson.

"I came up with the money but I have to go get it, where's the product?"

"Alright let me holler at my mans and them."

Tyson and Big Willie walked back to their cars. Tyson stood at his drivers door pulled out his cellphone and called Tonya. He told her tat he loved her and would see her tonight. Then yelled out to Big Willie, "The deal is set. My peps want it to go down in a couple of hours, how that sound?"

"Good, where and what time?"

"We will call you and give you the location and time. They very safe about it man."

"I understand." Big Willie replied as they go back into their cars and drove off in different directions.

- - - - -

Agent Johnson and Patterson arrived at the Federal building down town hours later and was approached by Agent Sims.

"Agent Johnson can i have a word with you, sir?"

"Yea what can I do for you, Sims?" Johnson knew that Sims was the mole.

"A Ms. Butler and her client Joey Knight came to talk to you. But I was unable to help them because I don't know what's going on. But she did leave her number for you to contact her." Sims wiped his nose with a used snot rag before pulling out a piece of paper with Ms. Butler's number on it.

"How long they been gone?"

"About an hour and a half." Sim's replied looking around Johnson's office while Patterson stood by the door.

"Umm Patterson get Ms. Butler on the phone for me." Johnson handed Patterson the phone number.

Patterson waked over to Johnson and grabbed the phone number our of his hand and picked up the phone to dial the number. The phone rang but he got her voicemail so he left a message.

"If you don't mind could you enlighten me on what's going on sir?" Sims asked Johnson.

"Well this kid named Joey Knight is wanted for questioning in the murder of Mike Wilson. However, the witness who identified him is now also dead. And the murder weapon was found at Tony Sloan's mother's house with his fingerprints. So we just need to clear up a few things with Mr. Knight. To be honest I don't think he knows anything but I still want to question him." Johnson replied knowing Sims would report back to Gomez.

Johnson got up from his chair, "Let me know if they return the call or come in but right now I have a meeting with the chief." Winking his eye at Patterson.

"Yes sir, I'll keep my ears and eyes open." Some replied walking out of the office to get on the phone with Gormez.

Agent Johnson waited for Sims to leave the office then turned to Patterson, "keep an eye on hime, he's the mole and I just set the bait."

- - - - -

Dantwan pulled up on the block jumping out of his truck like the task force. He had a black steel bat in his hand with a tie tucked in his waist line. He walked over to Tuna who was standing at the Deklsa night club, "Where he at?"

"I don't know where he went, he was just sitting right there, down on the black top." Tuna replied pointing in the direction where Mark was sitting a few minutes ago.

Dantwan then shouted down the block and Sperm head came running up the street, seen it was Dantwan and thought that he was back with more product.

"What's popping little nigga, you going against the grain?"

"What you talking about nigga, I'm NTP to the heart."

"What you doing selling for somebody else then nigga?" Dantwan stepped to Sperm head ready to beat him down with his bat.

"Nigga please you know front shit is ho shit. That nigga was blessing a nigga so I cop from him because he was out and you wouldn't return our call. We missing this paper."

"What numbers nigga?"

"Shid, I'm copping an ounce of med for five hundred dollars." Sperm replied pulling out a knot of money.

"Say word."

"Word to a mothafucka but I think he must have came into some work and trying to get it off quick."

Dantwan knew then that Mark had to have robbed Chop then killed him.

" I can't knock your hustle, coming across a deal like that I would have done the same thing." Smiling at little soldier, "Well where did he go?"

"He said he would be back. He said he had to go re-up."

Dantwan told Sperm and Tuna to follow him to his truck. He pulled out a back pack and handed them an ounce of cooked up cocaine, "Bring back the same thing but when that nigga come back through and I'm not here rob him and split the profit. Cop from me and I'm going to superman bless ya."

- - - - -

Paula had been waiting at the ing mansion in Mexico for Mr. Gormez. She was told that he would be returning in a second which turned into hours. Paula felt that something was wrong because of the way the bodyguards and family members were moving around the mansion nervously. Paula was then escorted to a large bedroom by two bodyguards. paula sat down on the bed then laid back and dozed off. She was waken an hour later by Gomez cussing and fussing like a drunken whore.

"Hold down your voice honey before you wake up Paula." Peggy stated.

Paula eased down the stairs and peeped around the corner into the large room where she saw Peggy and her uncle with four other men talking. Gomez paced the floor as his phone began ringing. He answered and shouted into it for about 2 minutes before slamming the phone down.

"Boys that was agent Sims and I believe that we have found one of the men responsible for the robbery and death of our family members." He stated as his phone began ringing again, "What!" He shouted.

Gomez talked on the phone for another five minutes but this time he was smiling ear to ear, "Boys it's getting better and better by the minute. That was Heinz, he has another one to add to the list."

Gomez went on to tell his lieutenant what information he just received and that he wants Joey and Tyson six feet deep by tomorrow night. Paula's mouth dropped as she wondered why he wanted them dead.

"Them son's of bitches killed Pedro, Julio, Paps, and they took my coca and heroin and over a million dollars from me. And now they are going to reap what they sowed.

Paula stumbled back hitting the wall and the sound caught everyone's attention. The lieutenant immediately pulled his weapon and aimed at the door. Paula took a deep breath and walked into the room rubbing her eyes.

"Hey Sunshine, did I wake you?"

"No I was getting up anyway." Paula then turned to Peggy, "Hey Peggy."

"How are you doing Paula?" Peggy asked standing up to hug Paula.

"Where's Shantez at?"

"Sit down sunshine. I have some more bad news to tell you." Gomez stated grabbing her arm and rubbing her hand as he guided her to a chair. He told her that Shantez was murdered last night and the ones responsible will pay with for it.

"When and where was he killed?"

"Last night in Idaho."

So at this point Paula knew that Joey and Tyson didn't do it because she was with them at the club the whole night. Paula then thought about how Tyson and Joey disappeared for two hours but immediately erased that thought because she saw them go into an office at the club.

"Is this what you called me her for Paps?"

"Yes Sunshine, I didn't want you to be alone when you got the news. I want you to be around family."

"Thank you Papa. But I have to return to the states. I only came because I thought something else was wrong with you."

Peggy rolled her eyes and sucked her teeth at Paula request to leave. Gomez then asked the lieutenants to assist Paula with anything she needed and escort her back to the private jet. One hour later Paula was back on the jet to Greenville South Carolina. She arrived at the Donaldson center private air strip two hours later.

# CHAPTER 34

Debra, Joey, and Reader sat the cafe waiting on Debra's guest to arrive. Debra looked down at he Jacob's watch, "My friend will be here any minute now."

Two minutes later a familiar brown skin brother steeped through the cafe door. He had wavy hair, had on duck head shorts with a shirt and socks to match. A gold Rolex and bracelet draped his wrist while a wedding ring covered his finger. He also word a diamond cut rope with a symbol of the star of David around his neck. The necklace was handed down to him by his late father, Walter Michael Jones.

"I see we have company." Dyson stated pulling his chair out preparing to sit down.

"What's happening old school?" Joey spoke.

"A little bit of this and a little bit of that." Dyson replied as he kicked Debra under the table because he didn't like the fact that she had invited guests to their private spot.

"Boy you crazy, I took the liberty of ordering your favorite." Debra looked at Dyson.

"Thank you baby girl. Now what brings you two to my private meeting?" Dyson asked looking at Joey and Reader with his hands folded on the table.

"We just came from the Federal building and decided that we wanted something to eat. And since I had to meet you here we might as well eat here. Been sitting here over an hour waiting on your late ass." Debra chimed in.

"Excuse me, I have to take this call." Joey excused himself from the table.

"Damn you look very familiar." Dyson asked Reader.

"Boy don't even act like you don't remember me, nigga."

"For real where you from?"

"Boy all them damn packs I use to slang for your ass." Reader voice got louder causing Joey to turn around to make sure everything, alright.

"Hold that shit down!" Dyson shushed Reader.

"I told you, you don't get away with nothing, you just get by." Debra laughed.

Dyson took a closer look at Reader. Girl it's good to see you, especially well."

Debra didn't know what Dyson meant by Reader being well but didn't bother asking.

"How long as it been since I seen you?" Dyson asked.

"I see you the other night at the party."

"So you back in the clubs again?" Debra asked Dyson.

"Special event."

Joey walked back over to the table and sat down, "I apologize but we have to leave. Important business." Grabbing Reader by the hand to escort her out.

"Well, Mr. Knight I'll catch up with that agent later and I will keep you posted. Debra stated standing up to shake Joey and Readers hand.

Dyson stood up and gave Joey and Reader the NTP pound and hug, "Tell Ty to call me." Dyson's eyes followed Readers ass as she walked off.

"Stop boy, I'm going to tell your wife, Kim." Debra smirked.

"Yea I almost forgot about her." They both laughed.

- - - - -

"I want their entire family put down like wild hogs." Gorez shouted with his fist raised in the air bringing it down on the table.

"Yes sir." One of his men replied. He had been waiting on Gomez to call him into action.

"Everybody thinks you're dead so now its your time to shine big boy."

"I wont fall you sir."

Gomez handed the hit man a piece of paper with Joey, Dantwan, A.J. and Tyson's names on it. The hit man tucked the paper into his pocket and left as quickly as he came.

"It's all set in motion now." Gomez laid back in his lazy boy chair with his hands folded around his big belly.

- - - - -

Mark appeared back on the block thirty minutes later. Tuna

called Dantwan on the phone. Tuna and Sperm head tried to cop from Mark but Mark told them that he didn't have anymore work and flexed his gun just in case they tried something.

Dantwan arrived in under five minutes. He hoped out of the truck with a baseball bat and proceeded towards Mark.

"Yo Dee old boy got a strap on him."

Dantwan flashed his desert Eagle that he had under his shirt as he continued towards Mark. Suddenly his cellphone rung stopping him in his tracks. Joey was calling from the emergency number.

"What's so important?" Dantwan answered with base in his voice.

"What's going on with you now?" Joey asked picking up on the anger in Joey's tone.

Dantwan explained what he was about to do and who he was about to do it to.

"Let that be, we'll handle that later. We got more pressing matters to handle. So you and A.J. report to the Safe Haven immediately."

Datwan turned around and headed back to his truck.

"Yo Dee what's up?" Tuna asked confused.

"All dogs have their day and today is not his."

Dantwan and A.J. rode to the Safe Haven. Dantwan rolled A.J. in his wheelchair into the house with the rest of the family.

"Glad y'all could make it." Tyson said patting he top of a folder that sat in front of him.

"What done happened now?" Dantwan asked as he position A.J.'s wheelchair under the table.

"Well today we are getting ready to get rid of a key of heroin

for one hundred thousand dollars. Big Willie has agreed to buy it."
Tyson announced.

"Hold up Ty, Big Willie's connections are Mexicans. What if those are the same Mexicans we robbed from. They gone know their product."

"I know Dee but as always I have a plan. Listen carefully because I'm only going to say this once and then we're leaving to meet up with Big Willie.

Tyson then told the family his plan.

"Boy you sure do come up with it don't you?" A.J. said smiling.

"So y'all ready?" Tyson asking standing up from the table. "Follow me into the next room."

Tyson hit the button on a remote and the floor board slid back exposing every type of weapon imaginable. Each member grabbed one of their choice, then followed Tyson out to the garage. He had two black vans, two motorcycles and a couple of cars in the car port. Reader got into the driver seat of one of the vans while Joey got into the passenger seat. A.J. helped Dantwan into the back of the van. Dantwan and Tyson got into the other black van. The team pulled off and headed to meet Big Willie.

# CHAPTER 35

Ms. Debra Butler called Agent Johnson back after her lunch with Dyson. They sat up another meeting for the following morning. After John hung up the phone he was scratching his head, still trying to figure out how Joey fit into the scenario. Then he wandered if Agent Patterson found anything out about Agent Sims when suddenly Patterson walked into his office.

"We need to talk but we can't talk here." Grabbing Johnson's members only jacket from the coat rack and tossing it to him.

Johnson grabbed his keys as they walked out of the building to his car. As they sat in his car, Patterson put his index finger up to his mouth. Signaling to Johnson not to speak. So Johnson drove off and they rode in silence to the closest Apple Bee's parking lot on Augusta Road. They went sat in the back away from other guests.

"I overheard Sims talking to someone on the phone providing information about four people, and one of those people were Joey Knight."

"Would those names happen to be, Andre Johnson, Tyson Jones, and Dantwan Williams?"

"Yes sir, how did you know?"

Johnson had discovered Tyson's name in an interview with Ms.

Hills. His name was also mentioned by Raymond Hall's wife as a close friend of her husband. Then again at the night club where he was able to put the name with a face. Johnson began putting the pieces of the puzzle together. Tyson had agreed to give Joey the message to contact him so that meant Tyson knew him well enough. Plus the fact that he saw A.J., who was arrested for the murder of Mike Wilson and released on bond, factored in. And it was safe to assume that hot head Dantwan was up to no good. Johnson knew that the four boys were friends and more than likely had something to do with all the murders thats been going down around town.

"I think I know what's going on." Johnson said while taking a sip of his lemonade.

"What's that?" Patterson looking out the window at two cars pulling up.

"Shantez who's probably dead by now, said that Gomez nephew was robbed and murdered in a stash house. The men responsible took a million dollars and a lot of drugs. And that was the same stash house that Chris Hill's body was found next to Pedro's, both with bullets from the same gun."

"Find the gun, we find the killer."

"No that wouldn't make a difference. We got the gun but the finger prints belong to Tony Sloan and he was found dead already." Patterson looked around the restaurant, gathering his thoughts, "We are going to have to let this play out." As he looking out the window at two black males getting out of a chromed out whip.

"Sir we're going to have a lot of dead bodies."

"Look the solution to this problem is catching Jesus Gomez.

254

We need to inform them boys that their lives are in danger."
Johnson replied standing up from the table leaving a two dollar tip.

- - - - -

Paula sat around in her condo trying to get in touch with Joey. She couldn't allow her uncle to kill him. She reached for her cellphone and tried his number again. *Shit!* It went straight to voicemail. She grabbed her keys and jacket and jumped in her jeep to go find Joey.

- - - - -

The NTP family arrived thirty minutes early at the Sirrine stadium to meet with Big Willie. A high school football rally was taking place so people were everywhere. After the NTP family took their position, Tyson pulled his cellphone from his hip and dialed a number.

"Hello." Ricka Garoros answered.

"The eagle is about to land."

"Si."

"As we discussed."

Ricka was pulling into the stadium parking lot with two bodyguards with him as Tyson watched from his position. Tyson then made another phone call to Big Willie as he left his position to meet Ricka.

"Yeah."

"We are ready, you?"

"Sure where?"

Tyson gave Big Willie the location. Big Willie was ten minutes away with Heinz. Heinz called Gomez who had flown back into the states shortly after Paula. And of course Gormez wanted to be there so he ordered ten men to accompany him on the mission.

Big Willie and Heinz pulled up ten minutes later followed by three black vans escorting Gomez and his men. The men exited the van and took their positions. Big Willie and Heinz stood across from Gomez.

A.J. sitting in one of the NTP vans sat watching as Gomez men positioned themselves. He called Tyson to let him know that Gomez showed up. Tyson suspected that he would and told A.J. to let the rest of the family know.

Tyson called Big Willie back.

"Yea we're here." Big Willie said.

"Good, go to row A7, we'll make the transaction there." Tyson hung up the phone as he approached Ricka.

"How are doing friend?" Ricka asked.

"We getting ready to meet them now, where's the product?" Tyson asked.

Ricka's right hand man approached Tyson and placed a bag at Tyson's feet. Tyson took the key and a half out of the bag and put it into his back pack. Then told Ricka to follow him as he began walking to section A8 where they took a seat as if they were watching the game. One of the teams made a touch down and a crowd of people jumped up in celebration, causing Ricka to panic.

"Calm down, I got you." Tyson smirked as he spotted Big Willie, Gormez, and Heinz approaching.

Tyson looked around for Reader and spotted her close by dressed like a school cheerleader carrying an identical back pack as his. Tyson stood up as the men came closer, "They're here, stay put until I call you."

As Tyson made his way through the crowd, Reader made her move towards him with her back pack in position. As they crossed paths Reader and Tyson made the switch. Reader walked a way with Ricka's heroin then handed it off to Joey, sitting in the crowd dressed up like a fan with make up on his face, bare chested with a huge zero on his chest and back. Joey went back to the van and stashed the drugs under the seat in a secret compartment.

Tyson met Big Willie, Heinz, and Jesus in the food court.

"What's happening Will?"

"Everything is everything."

"Where's the money?" Tyson noticed Big Willie's hesitation told Big Willie, "My people with the scopes are watching."

"Well, when do we get to meet your people? I'd like to buy three more bricks if possible." Gomez stated in disbelief that Tyson was the mastermind of the operation.

Tyson then knew for sure that Gomez was the major drug lord who they robbed. So his intentions was to take Gormez to meet Ricka in an attempt to shift the blame.

"I don't believe that will be a problem but first we need to see the money and make the transaction." Tyson stated dropping the back pack of heroin by Big Willie's feet.

Big Willie grabbed the suit case from Heinz and gave it to Tyson. Tyson immediately began walking off as Heinz dug into the back inspecting the heroin.

"Yep, this is our man." Heinz stated.

"Kill that son of a bitch." Gomez stated as Tyson began

waiving at Ricka to come to him.

"Hold up." Big Willie stated, stopping Heinz from pulling his gun out.

Gomez watched two other men approach Tyson. Tyson told Ricka the men wanted to buy more bricks as he turned around and pointed towards Gomez. Tyson stepped behind them with the suit case full of money. Ricka and his man began walking towards Gomez as Tyson followed behind them. Dantwan walked by them heading in the opposite direction and Tyson handed the briefcase to him.

Ricka noticed that Tyson no longer had the money, "Where's the money?"

"I had it placed in the car as we planned."

Ricka continued to walked towards the men as him and Gormez's locked eyes. Both of their mouths snarled up like wild dogs. Gomez and Ricka jumped into action pulling their weapons and firing at each other. Big Willie began to reach for his gun when he was side swiped by Reader holding a 380 handgun. Reader stuck the gun to the side of his temple and squeezed the trigger. The crowd went crazy. People running and ducking. Heinz tried to reach for his gun but was hit with a double barrel shot to the back blowing his chest out by Joey.

As Gomez and Ricka stepped towards one another Joey picked up the other back pack and disappeared back into the crowd. Tyson took cover behind one of the food stands as Gormez's men appeared from every direction. Two shots from Ricka's gun sent Gomez to his knees. Then Ricka fired another shot to Gomez face and he fell face first to the ground. Ricka then tried to run but was met by Gomez hitman  who rearranged Ricka's entire face with a cop killer, killing him instantly.

People scattered like the roaches in Jackie Tucker's apartment. Dantwan and Reader high tailed it back to the van where A.J. and Joey was waiting smiling ear to ear.

A few moments later police was everywhere but Mr. Gormez's hitman disappeared into thin air along with Gormez's other men. Ricka was dead. Gormez was taken to the hospital while Tyson was taken down town for questioning.

A.J., Dantwan, Reader and Joey went back to the Safe Haven and discussed everything that took place before Joey called Butler and associates to get Tyson out of jail. But Debra was already on the case in a meeting to arrange Tyson's bond.

"My services have already been paid for by Tyson. But in the meantime get ready for your meeting tomorrow with Agent Johnson." Debra stated.

"Dantwan and A.J. I need y'all to go to Lisa and Karen's apartment until I call y'all later with further instructions. Reader I need for you to get twenty grand out the suitcase and follow me. I'll explain everything on the way." Joey ordered the family.

Joey and Reader hoped into Tyson's black crown vic and arrived at Gigges Bond Company twenty minutes later.

"Hello what can I do for you sir?" A white man with blue eyes asked Joey.

"Is John in?" Joey asked placing his hand on the counter.

"Yes I'm John."

"A friend of mine,Tyson told me to contact you if he ever went to jail."

"No problem, Tyson is a good friend of mine. I'll do anything in the world for him except kill myself." John laughed.

Reader placed the twenty grand on the counter.

"That's not necessary the bill is already taken care of." John said. "Hold up a minute let me call down to the station to see what his bond is." John made a phone call and within a few minutes he had information. "Tyson wasn't arrested, just taken in for questioning. But if he gets arrested I'll be the first to spring him."

"Thank you for your time John." Joey exited the office wondering how the news spend so fast regarding Tyson.

# CHAPTER 36

Paula rode back to Joey's condo and decided to wait for him since he wasn't answering his phone. She has to tell him about her uncle's intentions to kill him and his friends. Paula realized that she was in love with Joey and would do anything to prevent the demise of his existence. She walked into the bathroom and got into the tub for a hot bath. She noticed she coconut oil on the sink counter so she mixed it with her bath water. She eased into the hot water soaking her body as she thought about how her uncle claims Joey murdered Shantez. She knew it couldn't be possible. She couldn't figure out what the connection would be since Shantez spent most of his time in Texas.

Suddenly Paula heard the front door slam shut. Joey and Reader had returned. Joey felt a vibe that someone was in the condo or had been in the condo. So he pulled his gun and eased through the apartment as Reader pulled her gun too.

Paula got out of the tub and grabbed a towel to wear around her body. As she walked out the bathroom and turned the corner into the living room she was faced with two nines. Paula immediately threw her hands up to shield her face which cause the towel to drop.

"Girl is you crazy. I could have shot you!" Joey shouted out. He was seconds from blowing her face off.

"Yall sure are jumpy." Paula exhaled as she caught her breath.

Reader put her gun away and walked towards the kitchen to fix her a drink as Paula and Joey went into the bedroom. Reader walked in on Paula telling Joey what she heard her uncle tell his men.

"Reader call Dantwan and A.J. and tell them to go to the Safe Haven and stay there for the night." Joey ordered.

Reader left the bedroom, walking towards the living room to call A.J. and Dantwan. Five minutes later she walked back into the bedroom to Paula being sleep in Joey's arms. So she laid down on the bed next to them with her head on Joey's chest listening to his heart as they drift off to sleep.

- - - - -

Mark was walking down Rebecca Street in Nichol town when a red truck pulled beside him. Mark looked over his shoulder at a white man who looked familiar. The white man rolled down his window,

"You working?"

"What's happening? What you need?" Walking towards the car.

"Get in on the other side. I don't like doing business in the open.' The white man said as Mark walked around the truck and got in.

Mark and the white man pulled off and began riding around the block. Mark pulled out a pack of crack from his pants, "What you trying to spend?"

The driver refused to answer Mark and kept driving. Mark started to panic and reached for his twenty-five until the man pulled over on the side of the road.

"I really don't want no drugs, I want something else."

"Nah I don't get down like that man." Thinking the man thought he was a prostitute or something.

The man began laughing, "Nah it's not like that. I just want some information."

"What type of information?"

"I'll give you five hundred dollars if you can take me to any one of these guys. Joey Knight, Tyson Jones, Andre Johnson or Dantwan Williams." Flashing the money.

"Well I dont' know a Joey or Tyson but I do know Dantwan Williams and Andre Johnson and I know exactly where they at." *Payback's a bitch!*

"Five hundred now and two hundred if the location pans out"

Little did Mark know, he was feeding information to Gormez's hitman who wasn't known to leave any witnesses.

- - - - -

Gomez was in the hospital attached to machines and tubes, healing from gunshot wounds. Gomez had been shot nine times. The bullet proof vest he had on saved his life but the gunshot wound that past through his cheek bone, shattered his jaw. He had to have plastic surgery.

A nurse walked into Gormez's hospital room to check his I.V.

and wrote down his vitals. Standing outside was five Federal agents waiting for Gomez to wake up so that they can read him his rights and haul him off to jail. Sara, as well as other concerned family members and friends called the hospital for visitations the Federal agents wouldn't allow no-one near Gomez.

Several of Gormez men waiting patiently in the shadows for an opportunity to rescue him but the hospital was crawling with agents everywhere including the two agents playing cards in his room.

Gormez opened his eyes and groaned as he moved his arm causing sharp pain to spread through his shoulder.

"Ol' big boy is up now." Agent Patterson stated to his fellow agent as he flipped an Ace card on the table.

"Where am I?"

The agents ignored Gomez and continue playing cards. Patterson pulled his cellphone from his hip and called Johnson to let him know Gormez was awake.

- - - - -

"Mr. Jones my name is Agent Johnson with the Federal Bureau of Investigation. I believe we met the other night after at the club, am I right?"

"Yea I thought I recognized the face." Tyson replied placing his hands over his crossed legs.

"Well Mr. Jones your name came across my desk on three different occasions concerning a case I'm working on. We're trying to connect some dots and that's where you come in at." Johnson stared at Tyson's face trying to read his facial expressions.

"I don't know why my name would come across your desk but I can assure you that I have not broken any laws."

"So tell me, what were you doing t the football stadium?"

"Watching the football game like everybody else."

Johnson blew a deep breath out of his nose, "Good answer. But check this out there has been a hitman hired to take out you and your friends. Do you know anything about that?"

"Who would want to kill me and my friends?"

"Do you know a Jesus Gomez?" Johnson again tried to read Tyson's face and body language.

"No I can't say that I've ever heard that name." Tyson looked straight in Johnson's eyes and lied.

"Well Gomez is a powerful drug lord from Mexico and for some reason he want you, Joey Knight, Andre Johnson and Dantwan Williams dead?"

Tyson stared off into space thinking about why Gomez would want A.J. dead and why Reader's name wasn't mention. The other conclusion is that the police didn't know who actually robbed Gomez so therefor Gomez didn't know who actually killed his nephew.

"Jesus Gormez is in critical condition, it would be in your best interest to help us help you. We know about the robbery and that your friend Chris Hill was involved. We believe that the rest of you were involved in one way or another." Johnson shouted to get Tyson's attention which didn't sit well with him.

"Hold up, drug lords, robbery. I don't know what the hell movie y'all reenacting but I have not saw it. This conversation is over until my lawyer shows up."

"Mr. Jones, we're just saying that you should help us help you." Johnson begged as Tyson stood up from his chair causing the other two agents in the room to move in quickly blocking Tyson.

"Are y'all charging me with something or am I free to go?"

"No charges yet, you can leave." Johnson replied as the agents cleared Tyson's path. As Tyson walked towards the door Johnson added, "Mr. Jones, one more thing, please inform Mr. Knight that we still have a meeting tomorrow morning and to show up on time."

Tyson walked out of Johnson's office into the hallway at the same time Debra Butler appeared.

"Sorry I'm late."

"It's nothing. They wanted to question me." Tyson replied as he grabbed Debra's arm guiding her down the hall to quickly exit the building before officer Johnson had reason to lock him up on the spot.

- - - - -

Five minutes after Debra and Tyson left, Johnson received a phone call from Patterson that Gomez was awake and raising hell. Johnson grabbed his car keys off his desk and rushed to Greenville Memorial hospital.

Once at the hospital Johnson flashed his badge to gain access to the private elevator to the ninth floor.

"Hello fellas." Johnson spoke as he passed several agents before stepping into Gormez's room.

Gomez was wide awake and sitting up in the bed verbally assaulting Patterson and Hudson as Johnson walked in.

"Oh here comes another little piggy." Gomez giggled.

"Hello to you sir and how are you doing today Mr. Jesus Gomez or should I call you by your first name Roberto?

Gomez looked at agent Johnson and said, Santana, excuse me Agent Johnson. It's good to see you again and all in one piece."

"Well I didn't want to be ripped apart by sharks."

"So what can I do for you and why are you holding me?"

Johnson reached inside of his coat pocket and pulled out several indictments signed but he US Grand Jury and handed them to Gomez, "You have now been served." Johnson began reading Gormez his right.

Patterson stood up and walked over to the bed, slapping cuffs on Gomez as agent Hudson pushed the wheelchair closer to them.

"Do you want to try to get in the chair or do you want us to put you in it? Johnson smiled ear to ear.

"Fuck you pig." Gomez snarled.

The agents grabbed Gomez's 300 pound body and tossed him into the chair causing him to moan out in pain. The agents rolled Gormez to the elevator down to the basement floor where a bullet proof van sat waiting. As soon as they reached the van, Johnson received a phone call from another agent.

"They're on to you." The agent quickly hung up. Causing Johnson to call for the back up van to pull up. The agents put Gomez in the second van as the first van peeled off in a the opposite direction. While Johnson and Patterson escorted Gomez to the federal holding facility the other van was attacked by

Gormez's men. Several agents were killed in the line of duty but Gormez's men came up empty handed. Once they reached the holding facility they had a nurse check Gormez's vitals before moving him to another facility out of state at the request of the US attorney general.

# CHAPTER 37

Mark and the hit pulled up in front of Lisa's apartment in Roosevelt apartments. The white man backed is truck into the parking space inside Lisa's court.

"Ok which apartment?"

"There they go right there coming down the steps headed to that truck." Mark smiled as he pointed to Lisa, A.J, and Karen walking to Dantwan's truck.

Mark then asked for the two hundred dollars but the hitman didn't respond.

"Cracker, I know you ain't tying to play me?"

The hitman reached to grab Mark but met Mark's twenty-five aimed at his face. The hitman pulled the latch on the side of the driver seat and leaned back as Mark pulled the trigger shooting out the drivers window. The hitman jumped into action and grabbed his nine miller meter silencer from the floor and let off two shots, one shot hitting Mark in the face ripping off part of his right ear. Mark was able to slightly open his door just as another bullet hit him in the face causing him to fall out the car.

The gunfire caught Dantwan, Karen, A.J. and Lisa's attention. They all pulled their weapons. They saw Mark crawling on the ground as the hitman got out of his truck. The hitman passed Mark and headed in their direction. With their guns pulled the hit man walked closer, in a casual fashion.

As he got closer, A.J. recognized the hitman and lowered his weapon, "Detective Hoffman."

Dantwan, Karen and Lisa lowered their weapons and holstered them into their waists. As soon as Hoffman saw them let their guards down he raised his gun and began firing. Dantwan and Lisa dove for cover behind nearby cars, A.J. was left wide open being that he was in a wheelchair. Karen dove in front of A.J. and took four slugs in her neck and chest killing her instantly. A.J. fired back at Hoffman but wasn't able to maneuver due to Karen's body laying across his. Hoffman let off two shots at A.J. splattering his brains all over Karen.

Dantwan peeped from behind a truck just as Hoffman finished off A.J. Then he made his move, blazing his guns. Hoffman turned around and raised his gun, aimed, and began shooting back as they walked towards each other. Dantwan took a bullet to the shoulder knocking the gun out of his hand and fell down to one knee. Hoffman walked closer and kicked the gun away from his reach. Then kicked Dantwan in the chin knocking Dantwan on his back. Hoffman placed his foot on Dantwan's chest, aimed his gun and fired.

As Hoffman was aiming to fire again, Mark creeped behind him emptying his twenty-five automatic into Hoffman's head sending him falling on top of Dantwan's body.

Just as Mark stood standing over Dantwan and Hoffman, Lisa jumped from behind the car and ran up on Mark firing all nine bullets into him, killing him instantly. Lisa stood over Marks body as police sirens blared in the distance. Lisa looked at everybody dead around her, panicking. She dropped the gun and passed out in the street. Lisa was a awaken by police when they arrived. They also handcuffed her and took her downtown for questioning. As the dead bodies were lined up and one body taken to the hospital, the crime scene was taped off, and the crowd that quickly came, left.

- - - - -

Joey, Reader, and Paula was awaken from their sleep by banging on the door. Reader and Joey immediately got out of bed and rushed for their guns. Joey told Paula to open the door as he stood aiming his gun at the door.

"Who is it?"

"Ty."

Paula unlocked the door to let Tyson in. Joey and Reader stood their with their guns drawn until they were certain it was Tyson and he was alone.

"We gotta move and we gotta move now." Tyson shouted pacing the floor.

"I'm going with you." Paula stated to Joey.

"No that's not a good idea. Just go home and I will send for you when I get situated."

"No!" Paula shouted with her lips poked out, tapping her feet.

"We don't have time for this." Tyson shouted.

Reader came back into the living room with jackets and coats, "Y'all can discuss this on the way out the door." Reader grabbed the keys to Joey's whip.

Tyson hopped back into the car with Debra as he instructed Reader to follow them. Twenty minutes later they arrived at Butler and Associates Law Firm where they had a quick meeting discussing their next move.

Tyson pulled Joey to the side letting him know that Debra is going to make sure that Paula makes it to a safe place but the NTP family needed to leave Greenville right now. He told Joey about the place the second house that he has for them to stay until things blow over.

"What's going on Ty?" Joey asked watching how nervous his partner appeared.

Just as soon as Tyson was about to explain about the hit taken out on them, Reader rushed over to them with tears in her eyes, handing Tyson the phone.

"Your wife wants to speak to you."

"What's wrong baby?" Tyson panicked as he put the phone to his ear.

"I have some bad news. Dantwan, Karen and A.J. are dead and Lisa was arrested for murder."

Tyson dropped the phone and walked out of the building. Joey seeing the shock on Ty's face followed behind him.

"What's wrong Ty?" Joey grabbed Ty and placed his hands on top of Ty's shoulder.

"All of them dead. They all dead, man." Tyson began to cry.

"Who?" Joey started to panic.

" Dantwan, Karen, and A.J. and Lisa in jail for murder." The men stared at each other with tears running down their cheeks. Reader cried as she held both of them in her arms.

# CHAPTER 38

Three months passed by like a blink of an eye. The NTP family buried their fallen soldier and celebrated the one that survived. Dantwan's recovery came out a hero in Lisa's eyes and Lisa in his.

The NTP family sat around the table at the Safe Haven discussing business as usual. The family grew over the last few months. Tyson tapped his spoon against a glass to get everyone's attention.

"What's on the topic of discussion today?"

"Well my uncle is to appear in court in a few weeks and they are talking death sentence." Paula stated with coldness in heart.

Since Gomez was incarcerated Paula had collected her one million dollar life insurance for Pedro's death, another million that her uncle gave her, and one hundred million that her mother left her in a secret account that she didn't know existed until Gormez went to jail. Paula went to visit her uncle every weekend because the NTP family wanted her to keep tabs on him. But Paula had her own agenda, she will soon become power of attorney over the Gormez family's properties and money. The Gomez estate assets totaled roughly four hundred million not including his Swiss bank accounts.

"Anything else on the discussion board before we leave to go eat some of that good cooking my baby prepared for us today at Tyson's house?"

"Yeah, what about Debra's attorney fees for Lisa's old and new cases?" Dantwan mumbled because his Jaw was wired shut from the gun shot that shattered his jaw.

"What did he say?" reader asked.

"He asked about my lawyer fees." Lisa chimed in who was now apart of the NTP family and pregnant.

Ever since Lisa show and killed Mark her temperament was short. Jus two weeks ago Lisa shot two girls in the knee caps because she thought they were pushing up on her man. Now she is facing an assault and battery charge. Reader and Paula had to persuade the girl with money to drop the charges.

"Lisa don't worry about the bill, it's paid." Tyson stated.

"Thank you, Ty." Lisa replied running over to Tyson kissing him on the cheek, making her way around the table giving every family member a kiss.

"Well this meeting is over. Let's eat!"

Everybody stood up and bowed their heads. Joey led the prayer blessing their fallen family members and gaining new ones.

"Ya Allah for all the believing men, women, and children. Especially A.J., Karen, who have passed on to the after life, may you have mercy on their soul and judge them lightly. From Allah we come to Allah we shall return."

- - - - -

Gomez received a natural life sentence instead of the death

penalty. But after two weeks in a federal prison, Gomez was found dead, having from a drop cord in the prison laundry room. The Federal government closed the case calling it a suicide. However the word is that Ricka Gararo's little cousin Spanky and his crew of young thugs strung him up in retaliation of his uncles death.

Shortly after this, Agent Johnson announced his retirement and planned on traveling the world with his family. Agent Patterson was promoted to head agent taking Johnson's title.

Agent Sims was rightfully indicted and convicted for leaking information and received twenty-five years in federal prison in Kentucky.

Sara went back to the old country and married a man named Megal Gonzales, who supplied heroin back in the day but sold his operation for one billion dollars. He wore a pinky ring that symbolized his bid in the industry and it stood as protection against all drug families. Years later Sara died but no one ever seen her body. Gonzales claimed that she was cremated per her wishes. Paula gain another 6.5 million dollar from Sara's death.

Shantez's mother, Peggy was found dead outside of Mexico with her throat split. Word was that she was involved with Ricka Gararos and was giving him information on the Gomez family.

Debra Butler still has her meetings with Dyson every Thursday at the cafe and has become two million dollars richer having the NTP family as clients.

The women in the NTP family began their journey as pregnant women going into mother hood. Paula and Reader were both pregnant by Joey and still living together as one happy family. Lisa and Dantwan are expecting their first baby and couldn't be happier.

Tyson proposed to Tonya after the NTP family dinner. Everyone had left for the night when Tyson and Lisa retreated to their bedroom. Tonya sat Tyson down to give him the good news. Tyson assuming that it was bad news stopped Tonya before she could finish her sentence and pulled out a Rey's Jewelry box and got down one knee.

"Tony you're my everything. Without you I can't breathe, see, or think. You make me enjoy life whether we have money or not. I can't not imagine living without you. will you be my wife?"

Tonya jumped from the bed into Tyson's arms like a wild mountain lion.

"Yes! Yes! Yes!"

The two kissed passionately as they held each other tight with tears in their eyes.

"Now what did you have to tell me." Tyson asked.

Tony smiled, throwing hints at Tyson about her being pregnant and every hint went over his head.

"Well baby, I've been missing my friend for the last two months. I went to find out why and was told that she would be gone for six months and when she returns, twins are coming too."

Tyson didn't know what Tonya was talking about but she continued with her hints until he got frustrated and demanded that she tell him.

"Baby I'm pregnant and we're having twins!"

Tyson jumped out of the bed doing the crypt walk then broke it down with the Harlem shake, yelling for joy. Then leaned in and planted kisses all over Tonya face neck chest.

"So what will we name them? Tonya asked.

"Well if its a girl and boy, Andre and Karen."

- - - - -

A black limousine arrived just as Shantez's brother, Jimmy stepped off his private jet. Making his first debut to the United States. He got into the limousine.

"How are you doing Jimmy?

"I'm good. I presume that you are Heinz's father?" Jimmy asked shaking the old man's hand.

"Barry." Heinz's father replied handing Jimmy a folder.

"So these are the men responsible for my brother's death?"

"Yes that's them. They call themselves the NTP family."

The limousine pulled over at the Greenville County courthouse twenty minutes later. Barry and Jimmy walked into the courthouse to the Judges Chamber. In the entrance of the Judges Chamber the name plate read, *The Honorable Barry A. Little.*

Jim was sent from Mexico. At the request of Jim's mother, Barry pulled strings to get Jim hired as a prosecutor.

"I'm sorry to hear about your brother." Barry said, pouring them a drink.

"No need to be sorry he was a weak man and deserved what he got." Jim replied taking the drink from Barry's hand.

"So how are we going to handle this family?" Barry asked.

Jim paced the office and walked over to a book shelf with a lot of law journals. He turned around and looked Barry in the eyes and snarled, "We are going to take it to another level."

Stay tuned for, "The Next Level"